The Runaway Horse

The Runaway Horse

Jane Ayres

The Runaway Horse
Copyright: © 2010 by Jane Ayres
Original title: as above
Cover and inside illustrations: © Jennifer Bell
Cover layout: Stabenfeldt AS

Typeset by Roberta L. Melzl
Editor: Bobbie Chase
Printed in Germany, 2010

ISBN: 978-1-934983-70-6

Stabenfeldt Inc.
225 Park Avenue South
New York, NY 10003
www.pony.us

Available exclusively through PONY.

Chapter 1

"I'll miss you, Holly. So will Samurai."

Holly pushed back an unruly strand of her long black and crimson streaked hair as she watched her younger sister groom their gentle palomino horse. She gave her sister a reassuring smile. "I'll miss you, too, Claire. But it's only for the start of the summer vacation, just a few weeks. It'll fly by."

She leaned her elbows on the stable door, letting herself be soothed by the regular, rhythmic brush strokes as Claire massaged and polished the horse's golden coat. She'd never been away from home before and she felt anxious at the prospect. She was protective of her sister. But since getting Samurai, Claire's confidence and independence had soared, and although Holly would worry, she knew that Claire would be fine without her. Plus it would be a new experience to go somewhere different. She would be staying with her Aunt Helena, who ran the Seashells Bed & Breakfast by the sea. And she would be spending time with her twin cousins, Anna and Sam, whom she hadn't seen since they were toddlers. They were both fourteen, a couple of years younger than she. She hoped they would get along together.

"Are you looking forward to seeing Anna and Sam's ponies? I would be," said Claire.

"Suppose so," replied Holly. "I feel safe riding Samurai but you know how nervous I can be around strange horses."

Claire giggled. "I'd take strange horses over strange people any day. Anyway, your riding has improved tons thanks to my expert instruction, obviously." Claire had enjoyed teaching her older sister how to ride. "What time is your train in the morning?"

"Just after ten," replied Holly, starting to feel anxious again.

"You'll have to text me with all the gossip," insisted Claire.

Holly laughed. "You bet I will."

"I want pics of the ponies, too. And the place you're staying."

"Okay sis. Hey, I went on Dad's laptop and looked at the Seashells B&B website. It looks pretty, and it's just a ten-minute walk to the beach."

"Well, if you and the cousins hate each other you can always spend your time on the beach reading a book and getting a suntan."

"If it's that bad I'll be on the next train home!"

Holly always felt unsettled when she was about to embark on a new experience. She liked a familiar, comfortable routine, which usually included lots of reading and walking, the occasional quiet trail ride on Samurai, keeping an eye on her sister and hanging out with her friend Jenni and her new pony Daydream. Jenni was totally preoccupied with Daydream right now, which was fine with Holly. She was used to being surrounded by horse-crazy girls, and they still found time to be together. When summer ended they would both be starting college, and relaxing, sunny days would be replaced with busy schedules of lectures and essay writing.

Holly slept fitfully that night, and when the alarm went off she had a muzzy head, which persisted even after she sat on the train to Seashell Bay, having said her tearful goodbyes to Claire and her Dad. She knew that part of the reason she had been invited to spend three weeks away was to help her Aunt Helena, if needed. With her Uncle Tyson in Germany on business and the B&B fully booked, an extra pair of hands would be appreciated. As she rested her face on the glass, watching the countryside speed past, she smiled as she recalled the big adventure she and Jenni had shared after she saw a golden horse on the balcony of an apartment complex, from the train on her way to town. The horse had turned out to be Samurai, and in rescuing him they had also met and helped Seth, the boy who owned him. She had first met Jenni on a train station platform. She smiled to herself. Trains had certainly turned out to be a catalyst to adventure for her in the past. Would this journey turn out to be the start of something equally exciting?

She was dozing when, nearly four hours later, the train pulled in to Seashell Bay station. The noise of the brakes and changing rhythm woke her with a jolt. She had arrived. The butterflies returned as she grabbed her bag and backpack and made her way to the exit, where Aunt Helena had arranged to meet her.

She smelled the sea air as soon as she stepped off the train and inhaled deeply. Tangy, fresh – and new.

"Is that her?" An unfamiliar voice pierced the air and she saw a young girl with short chestnut brown hair and deep green eyes studying her from the open window of a big blue station wagon with dents in the bumper. A cheerful looking middle-aged woman wearing a bright floral skirt and white tee shirt leaned against the hood, waving. She bore a striking resemblance to the photo her Dad had shown her at breakfast, in case she didn't recognize her.

"Aunt Helena?"

"Holly! Great to see you. Good journey?" Aunt Helena hurried toward her, enveloping her in a friendly hug and a heady citrus perfume.

"Yes, thanks."

"Holly, I'm sure you won't remember the twins. After all, you were a lot younger then. This is Sam." She gestured to the green-eyed girl eyeing her curiously. "And that's Anna."

Another brown haired, green-eyed teenager, who was slouching in the front seat, gave her a lazy smile. "Hi."

"Hi, there," said Holly, giving a friendly smile and wondering how she would be able to tell them apart. Why did they have to be identical twins? She climbed into the back seat with Sam who, like her sister, was wearing torn jeans and a pale blue tee shirt.

"Are you a Goth?" asked Sam abruptly.

"Sam, don't be so rude," scolded Aunt Helena, starting the reluctant engine.

"I was only asking a question, 'cause she's got streaks in her hair and she's dressed in black."

"That doesn't mean she's a Goth," added Anna.

Holly felt awkward, and the silence that followed was quickly filled by Aunt Helena's small talk about Holly's journey. Anna played with her phone while Sam looked bored.

While paying sufficient attention to her aunt to answer her questions, Holly gazed out of the window, taking in her new surroundings. Tree lined country roads were soon replaced by long tracks framed by wide-open space, and then they drove up a steep, winding hill to the cliff tops. Holly felt a thrill of pleasure at the way the sunlight played on the waves as they crashed on the rocks, and at the sweeping expanse of sandy beach. It was stunning. It had been hot and sticky on the train, and she looked forward to going for a swim at the first opportunity.

Following her gaze, Sam said matter-of-factly, "We're used to it. When you live by the sea, it loses its novelty value."

Holly was about to reply when she was distracted by the sight of a big, imposing house on their left, set back from the road. It was like something out of an old movie, exuding character and atmosphere.

"Creepy, isn't it," commented Sam.

"She's a Goth, Sam, she'd like creepy," Anna piped in.

"That's Sedgewick," said Aunt Helena. "It's been on that cliff top for centuries. It has quite a history."

"And not a nice one," added Sam. "All you need to know about Sedgewick is to stay away from there."

"Why's that?" asked Holly, curious now.

Anna turned in the front seat and stared gravely at Holly. "Because everyone knows that Sedgewick is cursed."

Chapter 2

"Here we are, home sweet home," said Aunt Helena as the car took a left fork down a back road before coming to a halt at the end of a sandy drive. "You are probably tired, Holly, so once I've shown you to your room, feel free to take a nap. Did you eat on the train? I'll make you a sandwich."

Holly liked Aunt Helena, who was her Dad's sister, and seemed to share his considerate nature. She was reserving judgment on her cousins, however, who had not exactly made a favorable impression.

Her bedroom was on the second floor, large and spacious, with a sloped ceiling and a huge skylight, through which the sun streamed. Tossing her backpack and bag on the bed, she stood at the window and looked out, admiring the view. It was breathtaking. Sea, sand, sky and, on the cliff top, Sedgewick. She shuddered, though she attributed that to the breeze that blew in through the open window. She tried to dismiss what Anna had said. Probably trying to scare me, she decided. Glancing downwards, she noticed a small paddock containing two black ponies, which she supposed belonged to her cousins. She found herself thinking about Samurai and Claire – and home. She took out her phone and sent a text.

When she had unpacked her clothes and eaten the delicious snack her aunt prepared, Holly decided to introduce herself to the twins' ponies. They were a friendly pair and trotted up to the gate when they saw their new visitor, hoping for tidbits. Holly smiled. "They're a bit more welcoming than my cousins," she muttered under her breath. She turned abruptly when she heard footsteps behind her.

"Oh, hey, Anna," she said blushing, wondering if her comment had been overheard.

"Sam, actually. But don't worry; people always get us mixed up at first. Strangers, anyway."

Ouch, thought Holly. She would try to make polite conversation instead. "Your ponies seem very sweet. What are their names?"

"This is Merlin. He's Anna's and he's better-behaved than Blackbird, his brother, but not as fast." Sam rubbed his whiskery nose and the black gelding slobbered on her tee shirt. "We've had them for seven years now." Holly thought the only way she could tell the ponies apart was that Merlin had a tiny white star on his forehead whereas Blackbird was completely jet black and had no markings that she could see. She wished she could find such a simple way to tell her cousins apart. Maybe they dressed the same as a deliberate tactic to confuse people.

"Seven years? So you and Anna have been riding for that long?"

Sam nodded. "Yeah, we had our first lessons on our sixth birthday."

"Wow." Unlike me, thought Holly, who only started less than a year ago. She was sure to make a fool of herself if she went out riding with her cousins.

"Anna loves Merlin," said Sam, "but she's ambitious and wants to be a professional rider. She's won lots of prizes for jumping, but she's kind of outgrowing Merlin now. How long have you been riding, Holl?"

Holly was tempted to say that her name was not Holl, which sounded silly, but instead replied, "Not long."

"Do you have your own pony?" asked Sam, with more interest than she had shown so far in Holly.

"Kind of. I share him with my sister, Claire. His name's Samurai, and he's a gorgeous palomino. Would you like to see a picture?" She took out her phone and scrolled down her picture file. "That's him."

Sam's face lit up. "Oh wow, he's stunning. You lucky thing."

And suddenly Sam was bombarding her with questions about Samurai – how old was he, could he jump, how long had she had him, did she have any more photos… Holly quickly realized that finally they had some common ground – maybe the only thing they would have in common. But it was a start.

"Can I see?" Anna's voice piped up behind them, and Holly noticed that there was a difference between the twins – Anna's voice was slightly more high-pitched than Sam's. She would have to find something in their appearance that would make it more obvious at a glance, though. Anna shared Sam's excitement about Samurai and Holly felt hopeful that they would get along, and that they would talk about other things. She had lots of questions about her vacation home. Then Anna said abruptly, "Hey, are we going for that ride, Sam? I want to take Merlin up by the woods, and get in some jumping, since we lost our schooling time earlier waiting for Holly's train."

Holly felt a bit hurt at this, but told herself she was being hypersensitive. She hung around for a while as her cousins tacked up, wondering if they might suggest she join them. But they mounted and set off down the cliff path, with just a, "See ya later," as they disappeared toward the gate. The didn't bother asking what her plans were for the rest of the afternoon, but it was too nice a day to sulk. The sun was still shining and the sea was beckoning to her, so Holly ran back up to her room, grabbed her bikini and decided to go for a walk on the beach. She strolled along the sand, dodging children playing with balls and building sandcastles while their parents sunbathed and swam in the clear water. It was still early in the season and it wasn't too crowded, especially when she found a quiet little cove tucked away at the far end. Apart from a group of boys investigating the tidal pools for crabs, she was on her own. Perched on a rock, she became lost in her own thoughts, musing over the events since her arrival. She felt as if she were in another world. As she gazed into the cloudless blue sky, her eye was caught by the house on the cliff path, the one they had passed earlier that day in the car. Sedgewick. From what her cousins had said, it sounded mysterious – and intriguing. She wondered who lived there, if anyone. She decided to ask later.

She could easily have spent hours on the beach,

strolling and swimming in the cool, blue water, but was conscious of the fact that her aunt might be worrying, so she set off back for the B&B. Her cousins were already home, and were helping their mother set the tables for supper outside on the patio. An elderly couple was strolling hand in hand in the garden and Aunt Helena explained that they were Mr. and Mrs. Cameron, retired teachers who vacationed there every year and almost felt like part of the family.

"That's the nice thing about running a B&B," said Aunt Helena. "Meeting people."

"And we get some odd people here," added Anna.

"Ignore Anna," replied Aunt Helena. "We get a variety of guests, young and old. Everybody is different and that makes it interesting. We have two more arriving tomorrow, and you'll probably meet our artist soon."

"Artist?"

Sam muttered, "Another weirdo, Lena Fallowfield. She's staying for a whole month."

"Lena is terrific, and she's quite a well-known landscape painter," said Aunt Helena, setting out the utensils. "Now, Anna, will you go and get the salad, please?"

Later that night, when she was getting ready for bed, Holly reflected on the day. It was pleasant gazing up at the stars through the skylight as she drifted off to sleep, quicker than she anticipated. After a restful night, she woke early to the sound of hoof beats outside. Dashing to the window, she saw that her cousins were already up and out riding. She couldn't help feeling left out, but resolved to keep busy, so she showered, dressed and went down to help her Aunt Helena serve breakfast to the guests. Holly was a capable cook, having gotten used to helping her father after her mother left them many years ago. She was just pouring fruit juice into a tall glass when she heard clip-clopping out in the yard.

"I didn't think Anna and Sam would be back so soon," she said with surprise.

"They won't be, not for at least an hour," replied Aunt Helena, smiling. "But I think you should come outside and meet our new guest."

Puzzled, Holly put down the glass as instructed and followed her aunt outside. Standing in the yard was a tanned, cheerful boy riding a plump strawberry roan mare.

"Meet Pumpkin," he said, grinning. "She may be small, but she's good-natured and quiet." He slipped from the saddle and handed Holly the reins.

"Yours for the next few weeks," explained Aunt Helena. "I borrowed her from the local farm."

Holly was momentarily speechless.

"Well, I know what my twins are like when it comes to sharing their ponies, and I want you to enjoy your stay here."

"Thanks, Auntie."

"No problem. Now, after breakfast, you and Pumpkin can get to know each other. Seashell Bay is a very safe place, so you can ride anywhere – except the marshes. There's a big sign up, warning you not to go any further when you see it, and I know you're a sensible girl, Holly. All the same, you will promise to stay away from there, as we don't want any accidents, okay?"

Chapter 3

Pumpkin had to be the most laid-back pony she had ever encountered, decided Holly as they sauntered around the paddock together after breakfast. Holly wanted to get used to riding the elderly mare in a confined space before venturing out for a trail ride, but she needn't have worried. She felt like she was relaxing in her favorite armchair as Pumpkin plodded along, her head bobbing up and down, making her long mane ripple. Holly was surprised that the little mare was even capable of galloping, but that suited her fine. When they had trotted and managed a tiny canter, she returned to the gate and dismounted, just as a car pulled into the drive. A harassed looking woman got out with a pale, moody teenage boy. Neither seemed very happy, but Aunt Helena greeted them warmly.

"Mrs. Clayton, it's nice to see you again. And how is Ross? Goodness, he's grown, and it's only been a year since you last stayed with us."

Ross glared and muttered under his breath, "And I never wanted to come back, either."

Holly watched them go inside, wondering why he was so miserable. She felt much happier now that she had Pumpkin to share her free time, so she got out her phone and took a couple of photos of the little mare, who obligingly made a face, showing her front teeth. Holly giggled as she sent them to Claire and Jenni with a short text.

As she wandered indoors to get a drink, thirsty from her exercise, Holly noticed a middle-aged, auburn-haired woman wearing paint-stained jeans and a bright baggy shirt working at her easel on the patio. She couldn't resist a sneak peek at Lena Fallowfield's work in progress. The colors were vivid and powerful, and Holly thought the artist evoked the real spirit of the bay and the rocks. But once more her eye was drawn to the building on the cliff top, at the far right of the canvas. Sedgewick.

"Intriguing, isn't it?" said Lena, following Holly's gaze. Holly nodded.

"That house has tremendous presence, which I would so love to capture."

"I think you've done a great job," said Holly.

"Thank you, that's very kind." Lena wiped blue paint from a brush with a piece of cloth and continued, "Seashell Bay is such a peaceful place, and the light is perfect for my work."

"It's my first time staying here," said Holly.

"Hopefully not your last," replied Lena. "I adore it."

What a contrast to Ross's attitude, Holly reflected. Just then, the sound of hoof beats in the yard made Holly look up, and Anna and Sam trotted past. Holly waved, eager to be friends, but they didn't seem to notice her. Trying to hide her irritation she kept on chatting with Lena, and when she looked up again the twins were heading off to the beach on foot, towels and swimsuits tucked under their arms. Were they deliberately trying to exclude her? Holly had never expected instant friendship, especially since the twins were two years younger than she, and she felt way older.

"Do you have any spare time this morning?" asked Lena, reaching for her pencil and pad. "If you don't mind, I should like to sketch you."

"Okay," replied Holly. "But will you do one of Pumpkin, too?"

"It's a deal." Lena smiled.

After she had finished, she handed the sketch to a delighted Holly, and it had a place of pride in her bedroom.

As the day wore on, the sun became too hot to do anything other than sit in the shade and read a book, which Holly enjoyed doing. Who cared about her stupid cousins, she told herself. At least everyone else here was friendly.

It was late afternoon when Anna and Sam returned. Aunt Helena, who had been busy in the kitchen, stopped them in the doorway. "I've run out of milk," she said. "So perhaps you two could ride into town and get some for me. And take Holly with you, show her the area."

Holly looked up from the book she was reading on her lounge chair.

"But we just got back," complained Anna. "And we'll have to get changed."

"Well, get changed then. It'll only take a minute," replied Aunt Helena, who wasn't going to take no for an answer.

"Okay," muttered Sam reluctantly.

Ten minutes later they set off together, Holly wondering if her aunt had really run out of milk or whether this was just a ploy to get the girls acquainted. Anna, impatient as ever, rode off ahead, but Sam stayed close to Holly, riding beside her.

"What do you think of Pumpkin?" she asked.

"She's very sweet," replied Holly.

"Yes, she's nice," agreed Sam. "We learned to ride on her. She's bombproof."

Encouraged by their first real conversation, Holly chatted about her own riding experiences and Sam listened with interest.

When they reached the local stores, Sam and Holly stayed with the ponies while Anna went in to get the milk. The day was cooler now and the sky had darkened. "There's a storm on the way," said Sam. "We get scattered thunderstorms this time of year. They're sudden and heavy, but then the ground dries again quickly and the sun comes back out. But the night storms… that's a different matter."

Anna hurried out and grabbed Merlin from Sam. "Let's get back before we get soaked," she said. "I hate getting my hair wet, and Merlin doesn't like the rain."

She pushed him into a trot and as soon as they reached the grass at the side of the road, she broke into a canter. Sam followed and Pumpkin, after some persuasion, managed a half-hearted canter, puffing as if to say, "It's far too hot for all this exertion." Holly was inclined to agree and found herself struggling to keep up. She was worried that if she lost sight of her cousins she would be unable to find her way back. Just as she was about to shout out, "Hold on, you two, give me a chance to catch up," Anna and Sam came to an abrupt halt.

"Darn railway crossing," muttered Anna. "The gates are coming down."

"It'll only be for five minutes, max," said Sam.

Holly reined in, relieved to take a breather, so she was astonished when she heard the sound of hooves clattering loudly on the road behind them. A horse careered past, reins hanging loose, stirrups flapping against his lathered sides.

As he overtook them, Sam shouted, "Oh no, stop him!" But the horse was riderless, and clearly in an excitable state.

"The gates will stop him," said Anna hopefully, turning Merlin in an attempt to block the horse's path. But the horse, panicking, swerved violently and instead of stopping when he encountered the heavy iron crossing gates, he simply increased his pace.

"He's going to jump," gasped Anna in disbelief.

"He can't – he'll be killed," said Holly.

They all watched, mesmerized, as the big bay horse gathered up his forelegs and leaped over the first gate, onto the railway tracks. But now he was penned in by the other gate.

"He's trapped," said Sam anxiously. "We have to do something."

"Like what?" Anna looked just as scared as her sister. The horse hesitated, unsure of what to do. If he stayed where he was, he would be hit by the approaching train, thought Holly. If he ran, in either direction on the tracks, his fate would be the same. The only escape route would be to jump the other gate, taking him off the tracks and onto the road on the other side.

"Maybe we should climb over the gate, and try to lead him to the side, to safety," suggested Holly desperately. But they could already hear the train coming, and as it drew inexorably nearer and nearer, her heart pounded in her chest. There wasn't enough time for that. There wasn't enough time for anything. In less than a minute, it would be too late.

Unable to bear it, Holly closed her eyes, hardly daring to look. She heard Anna scream and then the roar of the train as it sped past. Taking a deep breath, she opened her eyes… to see the horse landing safely over the second railway crossing gate and galloping off into the distance.

Chapter 4

"We have to go after him!" exclaimed Holly, still reeling from what they had just witnessed.

Anna wasn't so sure. "He's too fast for our ponies and he's already disappeared. How would we find him?"

"But he could catch his feet in the reins or a rabbit hole and hurt himself," Holly persisted.

"It could be a wild goose chase," said Sam. "It'd be better to call the police when we get back, alert them."

"That could be too late," replied Holly. "And I wonder what happened to his rider?"

The crossing gates had opened by now and Anna and Sam were riding through, side-by-side. Holly hesitated, but Pumpkin was already following them.

"Sam's right, we'll call the police as soon as we get back," said Anna. "It's the sensible thing to do." Even so, she seemed to be hesitating. They turned off at the crossroads but Holly felt uneasy. She halted a reluctant Pumpkin and turned to go back.

"What on earth are you doing?" asked Sam.

"I'm going after that horse," said Holly resolutely.

"You're crazy," said Anna.

"Maybe," agreed Holly, pushing Pumpkin into a canter.

"Holly, come back, you'll get lost," shouted Sam as she rode away from them.

But Holly was determined to find the runaway horse before he got himself into more trouble. What if he got hit by a car? What if he ended up on the edge of the cliff? There were too many variables – and all of them bad. And what about his rider? Maybe he or she was lying injured in a ditch somewhere. Or worse.

Holly tried to push these thoughts to the back of her mind. She had to have a clear head, focus on finding the horse. When he had galloped into the distance, he had disappeared so quickly that he must have turned off through the woods, she decided, so she would do the same. Her instinct proved to be right, and as soon as Pumpkin found a clearing through the trees she saw recent hoof prints in the damp soil.

"It could be a coincidence, Pumpkin," she murmured, "or we may have gotten lucky."

They followed the tracks through the woods and out the other side – straight onto another road. The tracks stopped and Holly didn't know where to go next. She was completely lost, just as the twins had warned her. Her impulsive desire to rescue the horse had achieved nothing. It would be dark soon and her aunt would be worried. She had to stay calm. Like her sister. What would Claire do? Then she knew. She let the reins rest on Pumpkin's neck and nudged the mare's sides.

"Home, girl. You know the way, don't you?"

Pumpkin stood for a moment, sniffing the air. Then she set off down the road, taking a sharp left to cut across a cornfield, her pace steady and assured.

"I hope you know where you're going," murmured Holly, but it made sense that Pumpkin, who had lived in the area all her life, would know her way around. As the light began to fade, Holly had to accept that Sam and Anna had been right. She should have stayed with them. She just prayed that the runaway horse was safe.

As Pumpkin's pace quickened, Holly assumed they must be getting nearer home. She wasn't looking forward to facing the "I told you so's" from her cousins and Aunt Helena's disappointment in her foolish behavior. But a high-pitched, distressed whinny intruded upon her thoughts.

"That wasn't you, was it Pumps?" she asked, already knowing the answer. She halted and listened, her ears straining. Did she imagine it? Then another frightened whinny cut across the still night air. Could it be the runaway horse?

"Come on, Pumpkin, we have to go and find him," she said, urging the mare to turn back. Pumpkin wasn't happy and fought for her head.

"Your dinner can wait," said Holly, finally managing to steer in the direction of the sound. But as they drew closer, Holly realized that Pumpkin's reluctance wasn't entirely due to greed for her evening feed. An ominous warning sign loomed up ahead and Holly felt her stomach quiver when she discovered where they were heading. The marshes.

"Of all the places in Seashell Bay, the railway gate-jumping horse has to end up here," she sighed. "I don't like this any more than you, Pumpkin," she continued, "but we have to help him."

Holly rode cautiously onwards as Pumpkin snorted

disagreeably, deciding that it would be safer on the mare, who was likely to be more surefooted than her human rider. But as soon as the ground beneath them became too soft and spongy, Pumpkin stopped and dug her heels in, refusing to go on.

"I don't blame you, girl," admitted Holly, dismounting, her own legs shaking. She gripped hold of the reins tightly, her boots sliding in the mud. She could see the bay horse now, thrashing in the slippery mire, his eyes panic-stricken. Her mind raced. What could she do to get him out? Clearly, she would have to use Pumpkin's strength, so somehow she must get close enough to the horse to grab his reins and attach them to her saddle. But how could she get close enough without endangering herself and Pumpkin? Distracted by the perils of the situation, she was taken by surprise when Pumpkin, sensing the potential danger they were in, threw her head and pulled the reins out of Holly's hands. Before she had a chance to grab them back, the mare had turned and was high-tailing it away.

"Pumpkin, come back!" yelled Holly desperately, but Pumpkin kept going.

For a moment, Holly was furious. So much for her supposedly bombproof pony. Samurai would not have deserted her like that. Then the fear hit her. She had a terrible choice to make now: protect herself by walking away from here and trying to find her way home, abandoning the bay horse, or stay and try to figure out a way to get him free. He had stopped struggling as much now, maybe realizing how futile it was. He was stuck solid, and without help she had little chance of rescuing him. Still, she wasn't about to give up.

"Easy, boy," she whispered. "I'll get you out, I promise."

Holly took out her cell phone, but she wasn't surprised when there was no signal. Her cousins had said that there were places in the bay and along the cliff tops where the signal cut out, and this was clearly one of them.

"Well done, Holly, you are lost, alone, and unless you can come up with a solution fast, you are going to watch this horse die," she rebuked herself sharply. Could things possibly get any worse? In the gathering darkness, she cast around for something, anything she could use to help the horse. But there were no trees or bushes to break branches from. There was nothing here at all. Just the marsh and the warning sign.

An idea came to her. The sign… it must be at least 6 feet high and made of strong wood. If she could pull it out of the ground, then lie it across the marsh, she could crawl along it and keep the horse's head up, above the mud. Maybe until help arrived, because the good thing about Pumpkin bolting was that when she returned home riderless, a search party would surely be sent out to look for her. But would the sign hold her weight? She had to get it out first. Carefully and slowly, Holly retraced her steps and grasped the base of the wooden sign firmly and pulled. But it wouldn't budge, not even an inch.

"Come on, move," she cried with frustration, but deep down she knew it was hopeless. She wasn't especially physically strong, and it felt like it would take Superman to uproot it. She glanced across at the horse and saw that the mud was now up to his neck. The gravity of his plight propelled her into one final, desperate attempt to lift the sign. Gathering all her remaining strength, she bent her knees and heaved with such force that she toppled over backwards – and straight into the marsh. Spitting out mouthfuls of the foul-tasting stuff she tried to get up but found she was stuck fast – just like the horse. Holly swore loudly, fighting down the panic that threatened to overwhelm her. This day was really turning out badly. There was only one thing to do now.

"Help!" she screamed as loudly as she could. "Help me!"

She called until her throat was hoarse. Why was she so stupid? Why hadn't she listened to her cousins? She was in serious trouble now – really serious. Even so, she had to somehow stay in control of her emotions. If this was a movie, she would be rescued by someone out walking their dog, right in the nick of time. But this wasn't a movie. And who in their right mind would be out by the marshes at night? She would have to rely on Pumpkin getting back and people rushing out to find her, before it was too late. Time stood still and she began to shiver, her teeth chattering. Her eyelids felt heavy and she wanted to close her eyes, to pretend this wasn't happening. Even so, sleep seemed a preferable option. Maybe this was just a bad dream. She must have let her eyes shut, just for a minute or so, because when she opened them, she saw a dark figure standing at the edge of the marsh. She blinked. She was definitely dreaming now. Then he spoke.

"Hold on, there, don't give up! I'm going to get you out."

His voice was strong and reassuring.

"Are you real?" Holly heard herself saying.

"As real as you are," he replied. "I'm going to throw you these knotted reins and you have to tie them around your waist. Can you do that?"

"Yes," Holly whispered.

"Good. Once you've got them, shout and I'll attach them to the saddle and Dynamite will pull you out."

"Dynamite?" she said, suddenly alarmed.

"My horse."

"Oh." A hero on horseback. What more could she wish for?

Minutes later, with the help of the stranger and his

horse, and with much squelching, the marsh reluctantly released her from its clutches and she lay on the ground, panting and exhausted.

"One down, one to go," he said matter-of-factly.

While she lay coughing and spluttering, he quickly assembled a makeshift lasso from reins and stirrup leathers and managed, after half a dozen attempts, to throw it over the bay horse's almost submerged neck. He fastened it to Dynamite's saddle and with much shouting and encouragement from the stranger and a superhuman effort from his powerful black horse, the bay's shoulders slowly began to rise. Realizing that he was being rescued, the horse suddenly tried to help himself, and once he had his forelegs free, struggled to scramble for the bank. When, finally, he was on safe ground once more, Holly wanted to cry with relief and gratitude.

"Thank you," she gasped.

"I hope your horse will be alright; he looks as if he's hurt his shoulder," said her rescuer, who she now realized was not much older than she was.

"He's not my horse," replied Holly, adding, "It's a long story."

"I live close by," he said. "It'll be best if you both come back with me and get cleaned up. We might need to get the vet to take a look at the horse."

He offered her his hand and she took a wobbly step

forwards, nearly falling over. Hastily he said, "I think you'd better ride my horse. I'll lead the bay."

"I'll make your saddle all muddy," she mumbled as he helped her mount but he just laughed. "I can clean it."

As they walked along in silence under the moonlit sky, Holly said, "I was very lucky that you happened to be passing. I didn't imagine anyone would be out around here."

"I often ride at night. I like the darkness," he replied.

Holly felt a tingle travel down her spine and she wasn't sure if it was from the cold or excitement – or sudden apprehension.

"We'll be home soon," he said. "It's just up on the cliff top."

Holly peered up ahead at the spooky yet familiar house outlined under a moonlit sky. She shuddered. The mysterious stranger's home was Sedgewick.

Chapter 5

As they passed through the big heavy iron gates, which shut behind them with an ominous clang, the boy said, "I'm Jordan, by the way."

"Holly," she mumbled, shivering.

"You'll catch a cold," said the boy, sounding concerned. "I'll stable the horses, Holly, while you go inside in the warmth. You can use the phone to call your folks and let them know you're safe."

"Thanks," she replied.

The inside of the house felt lonely and quiet. There were cobwebs across the light fixtures and the corners of the high ceilings, and everything had an air of neglect. The furniture was old and the big sofa and armchairs tattered. Dust coated the row of framed pictures on the bookshelf and across the grand piano that dominated the far side of the room. Holly could not get to the phone quickly enough. Aunt Helena answered after only two rings. She sounded worried sick. "Thank goodness you're safe," she said, after Holly explained what had happened. "I'll be over to get you right away."

After she put the phone down, Holly once more became aware of the silence and the chill in the air. Old houses got cold easily, she told herself, shivering, and a mud bath in the marsh wasn't exactly the best way to warm up. She wandered over to the bookshelf, her eyes drawn to the pictures of horses. She recognized Dynamite in one, with his distinctive white crescent moon in the middle of his forehead, standing beside a very pretty blonde woman with bright blue eyes and a warm smile. As she studied it, she felt cold breath on the back of her neck.

"That's my mother."

"Jordan, you made me jump," she said, springing away from him in surprise.

"Sorry. Didn't mean to." He looked embarrassed. "Are you okay?"

Holly nodded. "Just fine. Do you play the piano?"

"Not really. Well, I had a few lessons. It was my mother's. She played brilliantly." He sounded wistful, but then seemed to gather himself together again. "I called the vet and he's coming tomorrow morning. The horse seems calm now. I put him in the stable next to Dynamite."

"That's good. He's had a traumatic night."

"He's not the only one. I'm going to make some tea. Want some?"

"Yes, please."

She sank into one of the big armchairs and he soon returned with a tray and two mugs, some cookies and a bowl of sugar. Holly spooned in several teaspoons, not counting, unable to take her eyes off Jordan. The room was dimly lit by antique type standard lamps but she was able to get a real look at him for the first time. He wore denim jeans, now caked with dried mud, and a black sweatshirt, and his hair was jet black. There was something about him that she was drawn to. His voice, his looks, his polite, calm manner. Every inch a hero. But what was he doing riding out in the dark? And where were his parents?

"So, Holly, do you have the time to tell me your story?" he began as he settled in the chair opposite her.

"What story? Oh, you mean how I got stuck in the marsh with a horse that isn't even mine?"

He laughed. "I like a mystery."

Holly found herself telling him all about her cousins and the railway crossing drama and how her impulsive behavior had gotten her into trouble.

"I'm an idiot," she concluded, smiling sheepishly.

"Maybe," he joked. "But a caring idiot. And brave too, putting the horse's safety above your own. I wonder who owns him? Well, at least he's safe now, that's the main thing. He's had a terrible scare. And so have you." He sounded genuinely concerned.

She took a sip of tea and noticed how blue his eyes were. Deep blue. There was a mesmerizing quality about this boy. And he even made great tea.

"Dad's away on business and won't be back until late, so it's nice to have some company," he remarked.

The sudden, but majestic, sound of the doorbell was an unwelcome interruption.

"That could be your aunt," he said, getting up to answer.

Holly sighed. She was enjoying her conversation with Jordan – and his company. She almost didn't want to leave.

Aunt Helena thanked Jordan and then Holly thanked him, several times, before her aunt bundled her into the waiting car, and within minutes she was back at the Seashell B&B and comparative normality. It was wonderful to soak in a hot bath and remove all traces of the horrible marsh mud from her skin and hair. Aunt Helena had told her that when Pumpkin returned riderless they had all been terrified. And Anna and Sam, it appeared, had been given a good scolding for letting her go off on her own. They had also been worried sick – and, according to her aunt, Sam at least felt guilty.

Feeling exhausted now, Holly climbed into bed and looked up through the skylight at the stars. She was lucky, she reflected. She was alive and safe, and so was the horse, thanks to her handsome hero. A furtive knock on the door was followed by Sam's voice. "Are you awake, Holly?" she whispered.

"I am now," she replied.

"Can we come in?" and before she could answer, her two cousins had scurried into her bedroom and perched on the end of the bed.

"Come on then Holl, what did you think of Sedgewick?" demanded Anna.

"We warned you it was creepy."

"And you met Jordan? Mom said he rescued you," added Sam, "Though we both find that hard to believe."

"He saved me, and he was amazing," replied Holly defensively, wondering if they knew Jordan. They had not mentioned his name to her before. "And Sedgewick is just a big old house."

"Is that it? Come on, Holl, we want details. And lots of them. Nothing exciting ever happens around here," continued Anna.

Holly yawned. "I'll tell you in the morning."

"Spoilsport," retorted Anna sulkily.

"Did they find the horse's rider yet?" asked Holly.

"Mom called the police as soon as we got back and they're out looking for her. And then when Pumpkin returned without you, she was onto them again. A night of drama in Seashell Bay," joked Sam. "Come on, sis," she said to Anna. "Holly needs to get some sleep."

Anna shrugged. "Okay."

They all said goodnight and tiptoed out of the room. Just as Holly was about to close her eyes, Anna poked her head back around the door. "You've got guts, Holl, I'll give you that. Night night."

Holly smiled and minutes later she was fast asleep.

When she awoke seven hours later, she knew she must have dreamed about the bay horse, because he was the first thing she thought about. She got up and stared out of the window across the gull-speckled cliff tops – to Sedgewick. The place even looked mystical in the sunlight. She wondered if the vet had arrived yet. There were things she needed to know, and a boy she wanted to see. But before she could do that, her aunt insisted that she eat a good breakfast after her ordeal the night before, and she fussed over her like a brood hen, which seemed to amuse her cousins. She glanced over at the other guests as she sipped her orange juice. Lena Fallowfield was gazing into space, clearly happy in her own thoughts of canvas and landscapes, Holly decided. Lena smiled across at Holly when she noticed her staring. There was no such harmony between Ross Clayton and his harassed looking mother, as they appeared to be arguing over the table, her voice more raised than his. Holly heard him mumble, "I told you I didn't want to come back here, but you don't listen." There was a sadness in his voice that she found unsettling.

"So, Holly, give us the goods on last night's adventure," said Anna, spooning marmalade onto her toast.

"I got lost, as you said I would," replied Holly sheepishly, "but thanks to Pumpkin, I got back on track, and then when I caught up with the horse he was trapped in the marsh. I tried to rescue him, Pumpkin abandoned me and then I got stuck myself."

"Were you scared?" asked Sam.

"Are you kidding? I was afraid it wasn't going to be just my vacation that got cut short. I'm lucky to be here talking to you like this."

"Very lucky," agreed Sam.

"Thanks to the local hero," said Anna with an edge to her voice.

Holly was about to ask Anna why she was so anti-Jordan but her cousin had already gotten up, ready to go.

"Stable time," she announced abruptly. "Trail ride first, then we hit the beach. Come on, Sam. Want to join us, Holly?"

"No, thanks." Holly had other plans.

Anna shrugged. "Suit yourself. Have fun."

"See you later," said Sam. "Don't get stuck in the marshes again."

Holly relaxed back in her chair. The dining room was empty now and she savored the silence for a few moments. It was going to be a hot day.

Ten minutes later she was wearing jeans and a bikini and armed with a towel.

"Don't forget your sunscreen, especially with your delicate complexion," said her aunt.

"Already slapped on," grinned Holly.

She nodded a greeting to Lena Fallowfield, who had set out her paint and easel for the morning. Pumpkin was grazing nonchalantly in the paddock; she gave a cursory glance in Holly's direction before returning to her grazing.

"Deserter," Holly reprimanded lightly. "Leaving me in the marshes like that. Maybe I would have done the same, though, if I'd been a pony."

Pumpkin munched a mouthful of grass. "Well, you

can have a day off today," continued Holly. "I've got other things to do."

She set off in the direction of the beach path, breathing in the fresh salty air. But as soon as she was out of view of the B&B she changed direction, as she had planned.

It was only a short walk to Sedgewick up the cliff path, which was strewn with brightly colored wildflowers buzzing with honeybees. She was accompanied by summer birdsong, and when she glanced down at the sea below, she noticed the dorsal fin of a dolphin breaking the surface of the glistening water. As she approached Sedgewick, she could hear cheerful whistling coming from the stables. She wondered if Jordan had heard her footsteps because by the time she had reached the yard, he was already walking over to meet her.

"Hi, there." Jordan didn't seem surprised to see her and she thought from his friendly smile that maybe he was pleased.

"Hey." She found herself feeling strangely, and annoyingly, shy, standing there in her black jeans and halter neck bikini top.

"Did you sleep OK?" he asked.

"Like a baby," she replied. "How's the horse?"

"Pretty good," replied Jordan. "I'm just about to fill the hay nets. Want to give me a hand?"

Holly nodded. The bay horse was stabled next to

Jordan's black stallion, Dynamite, who jostled for attention as they passed by.

"He's gorgeous," commented Holly, unable to resist patting Dynamite on the neck, which rippled with hard muscle.

"He used to belong to my mom," said Jordan, and she thought she detected a hint of sadness in his tone. "And next to him is Mercury, who was my first horse. Retired now."

Holly glanced at the white-faced gray cob who was dozing over his half door.

"Hi, Mercury," she said softly, patting him on the nose.

"You'll be glad to know our bay visitor had a restful night and the vet saw him first thing and confirmed that his shoulder is bruised. Maybe he got hit by a car or knocked into something."

"Oh, poor thing. Will he be okay?"

"I'm thankful it's not serious," said Jordan. "He'll be stiff for a few days but no lasting damage. He's a nice looking guy."

He's not the only one, thought Holly mischievously.

The bay horse gave an enthusiastic nicker as he spied the hay. "He certainly has a good appetite," laughed Holly.

"And a name," added Jordan. "He's Trojan, and his rider was a vacationer, out trail riding."

"How do you know that?" Holly was impressed.

"The vet recognized the horse – turns out he's a recent addition to the Bretton Trail Riding Center, on the other side of the bay, so I called them after he left."

"That's lucky," said Holly.

"What do you mean?"

"That his owners have been found. They must be relieved."

"Not exactly." Jordan's tone darkened. "That trail riding center doesn't have a great reputation. I used to know someone who worked there and the horses aren't well cared for. Having this happen doesn't look good. I mean, if you were a parent you wouldn't be impressed if your daughter bolted and then went missing. Makes the riding center look really bad."

"True. Although we don't know the whole story yet, not until the girl turns up."

"Her family will blame Trojan or say the riding center was using a dangerous horse. Either way, Trojan's future doesn't look good."

Holly said adamantly, "We can't let anything bad happen to him. I'm sure it wasn't his fault."

"Let's hope they find his rider. What makes it worse, of course, is that it's her first vacation here so she doesn't know the area."

Holly frowned. That was bad news. She knew from

personal experience how silly it was to ride off on your own in unfamiliar territory. After all, she was just a vacationer, like the missing girl. She shuddered as she recalled her peril in the marshes. What if the girl had also ended up there?

"Hey, Trojan," murmured Holly, reaching out and stroking his soft muzzle. "If only you could tell us what happened last night."

The bright daylight gave her a chance to study him. He had big brown eyes and long eyelashes, a tousled black forelock and mane and a Roman nose. He seemed to have a gentle nature and, despite his trauma, was calm and relaxed.

"I think he likes you," said Jordan.

Her hand lingered on Trojan's face and her heart missed a beat when she considered how awful his fate could have been. She was glad she had pursued him, even though it was actually because of Jordan that they were both safe. Holly hesitated, wondering if she could pluck up the courage to ask Jordan if he wanted to go for a trail ride with her later.

"You can stay here as long as you like," said Jordan, "But I've got to go now. I have to meet Dad in town."

"Oh." Holly hoped she didn't sound too disappointed. "I'm sure Trojan would appreciate the company, though."

"I'll hang around here for a while then, if that's okay,"

said Holly. "I'll have three gorgeous horses to talk to – and a funny-looking bird."

Jordan followed her gaze. A large silvery gray bird with a black crown and a huge coral-red bill was perched on Dynamite's stable roof, resting what looked like a deformed leg. It had a round body, white face, blunt wings and short tail. "That bird is back again," said Jordan. "It's a Caspian tern, pretty rare for this area, actually, but it's been hanging around here on and off for months now. It especially seems to like Dynamite. I've even seen it resting on his back in the paddock, and he doesn't seem to mind at all."

Holly watched Jordan leave, wishing he could have stayed longer. This wasn't like her, she reflected. Boys had never really interested her, but maybe she had never met the right one? She sighed. He was gone and she would make the most of her time with Dynamite, Mercury and Trojan.

Mercury was gentle in contrast to Dynamite's more fiery nature. Even so, the black stallion was affectionate and enjoyed the attention she was giving him.

"You helped save my life," she told him gratefully, recalling how his strength had pulled her out and how he had calmly let her, a total stranger, ride him back to Sedgewick. "And Trojan's." She turned to the bay horse, who was resting his head over the half door of the stable.

"We both owe you a lot," she continued. "I hope you realize what Dynamite did for you," she said to Trojan, rubbing his ears.

After she had taken photos of the horses on her phone and texted them back to Claire and Jenni with a short message, Holly decided to walk back to the beach. The sun was warm and the waves splashed on the rocks. She would miss all this when she had to go home. She decided that when she graduated from college and got a job, she would save up and buy a house by the sea. She was lost in these thoughts when a familiar voice said sharply, "So where did you go?"

She peered over her shoulder and saw Sam and Anna lying on towels on the sand, having spent the past twenty minutes swimming and sunbathing.

Anna lowered her sunglasses and squinted through the sun at Holly. "Come on, Sam, three guesses. No, I bet I could get it in one," she continued. "Holly has been to see Jordan, I bet."

"You went back there?" asked Sam. "You're crazy."

"Why do you say that?" replied Holly.

"Holly likes Jordan, if you ask me."

"Well, no one did," snapped Holly.

But Sam was horrified. "Holly, you should stay away from that place. And Jordan."

"I don't see why I should."

"That house has a bad history," Sam persisted. "So has Jordan. He's nothing but trouble."

"You should listen to Sam," said Anna. "We're just giving you some friendly advice."

"It doesn't sound very friendly to me. You're both talking nonsense. Jordan is a great guy."

"If you think he's so perfect then just ask him what happened to his mother," snapped Anna angrily.

Holly was taken aback but also immediately intrigued. Sam went pale. "Enough, Anna," she hissed.

But Anna wasn't going to stop now. "He hurt Blackbird, too. Sam's pony is lucky to be alive, no thanks to Jordan."

Holly was astonished. Were they talking about the same boy?

Sam stood up and shook sand from her towel. "Enough arguing. If Holly wants to see Jordan it's her funeral. We tried to warn her." She tossed her towel back on the sand and strode off purposefully into the sea. Anna followed, leaving Holly standing alone.

Her mind reeling from the revelations, Holly walked back to the B&B.

She avoided her cousins for the rest of the day, curling up in the garden with a book instead, but she found it hard to concentrate. After supper, they sat in the lounge watching TV, with Anna and Sam sitting at one end and Holly at the other. None of them spoke.

Aunt Helena, sensing the tension, said, "Is everything alright, girls?"

"Fine," replied Anna.

"Holly?"

"Fine," she repeated, glaring at Anna.

Aunt Helena was considering whether or not to attempt to pursue the conversation – or lack of – when the local news report came on.

"*Police are increasingly concerned about the disappearance of tourist, Sarah Parker, who is still missing after falling from her horse while horseback riding.*"

Everyone listened intently, their arguments forgotten. "*Sarah has a heart condition and, without her medication, could be in serious danger.*"

"Oh no," breathed Sam.

The reporter continued, "*Anyone with any information, please call this number.*" Aunt Helena rapidly took the phone number down and turned to the girls.

"How awful. Her parents must be out of their minds with worry."

"We have to find her," said Holly.

"The police have been searching, and if they can't find her why would we have a chance?" retorted Anna.

"That shouldn't keep us from trying, though," replied Holly.

"You're right," agreed Sam. "But not through another

crazy, un-thought out rescue mission. We need to do it properly this time."

Holly was happy to let her cousins take charge since, as they pointed out, they knew the area and she didn't – a fact that had been painfully obvious the day before.

"Holly, you stick with me," said Sam, as they tacked up the horses.

"We should be able to get in at least two hours of searching before it gets too dark," added Anna.

As she and Sam rode over to the woods while Anna covered the sea paths, it crossed Holly's mind that Jordan would have been able to help them and been a good ally – but the way her cousins responded at the mention of his name, she decided against it – for the time being.

They scoured the woodland and the country roads, shouting, "Sarah," until their throats were hoarse. Before the sun went down, they all met back at the marshes, as agreed.

"No luck?" asked Anna, rejoining her sister and cousin.

Sam shook her head and they all shared a feeling of futility, which no one dared to voice.

"If she fell in the marsh…" Anna began slowly as they stared across the treacherous muddy plain.

"Don't say it," murmured Sam, shuddering.

They rode back reluctantly under the silent darkening sky. Holly doubted that anyone slept well that night, with the knowledge that Sarah Parker was spending her second night alone, lost and scared. Holly refused to believe the worst, although Anna's words still resonated in her mind.

At five a.m., Holly gave up trying to sleep and got up, dressed and took Pumpkin for a ride on the beach. It was deserted, unsurprisingly, and she rode undisturbed in the misty dawn light. It seemed so peaceful, she reflected, just her and the slightly sleepy little mare, watching the waves lapping on the sand. After a few moments, she became aware that she was not alone and smiled curiously at the large gray bird that had settled on a nearby rock and appeared to be watching her. As the lumbering bird moved, she noticed his deformed leg and bright red bill, and she recalled the tern that she had seen on Dynamite's stable roof. Surely it couldn't be the same bird? But there was something so distinctive about this one, and Jordan had said that Caspian terns were unusual in these parts. As she craned her neck to get a closer look, the bird soared upwards, hovering nearby before it flew away. She continued to amble alone and there, on the next rocky outcrop, was the tern again, as if waiting for her. When she had reached it, the bird took off once more, flying ahead. This pattern repeated, with an intrigued Holly following, until she realized that they had wandered off track and were in a secluded bay that she had not seen before. Not only that, but a heavy mist had descended, obscuring her vision. Holly paused, deciding what to do next. If she got lost again she would never live it down and her aunt might be more than a little upset with her. She would turn around and head back. The mist would lift as the sun rose, she told herself. But as she squeezed the reins, an eerie, ear-splitting screeching made her jump and Pumpkin shied violently, throwing her off balance and headlong into the soft, wet sand.

Still grasping the reins, she sat up, cursing the bird. When she blinked, it was gone, but instead, as the mist began to clear, she saw that she was sitting by the mouth of a large cave, partly obscured by rocks. Holly scrambled to her feet, looped Pumpkin's reins over a boulder and cautiously made her way inside, careful not to slip on the seaweed-strewn rocks. It smelled damp and strange, and she was able to walk upright without hitting her head on the cave roof. Despite her tentative steps, Holly still managed to slip and knock her ankle on a rock. "Ouch!" she cursed, bending down to rub it. That's it, she decided, enough exploring for me. Then she heard what appeared to be a low whimper, so faint as to be barely audible. She froze. What kind of creatures lived in sea caves? Bats, perhaps? Maybe a whole colony. Did bats make a sound? She held her breath, her heart thumping in her chest. There it was again. But this time, Holly felt sure it was human. But where was it coming from? She peered around frantically, but all the nooks and crannies that the cave harbored were too small for any person to squeeze into. Puzzled, she glanced upwards. That was when she saw the craggy ledge.

"Hello?" she called. "Is anyone there?"

Chapter 6

It was hardly a whisper, but Holly knew it was a girl's voice.

"Sarah? Is that you?"

There was no reply this time, so Holly grasped a jutting outcrop of rock, wedged her feet into a crevice and hauled herself up onto the ledge. There, curled up in a tight ball, was a disheveled girl, her long blonde hair wet and matted and her clothes damp and torn. "My head aches," she sobbed, peering at Holly through her tears.

"It's okay, I'm going to get you out," soothed Holly. She reached out and took the girl's hand, which was ice cold.

"I'm scared," the girl said, her teeth chattering. "Am I going to die?"

"Of course you're not," replied Holly briskly, sounding far more confident than she actually felt. Sarah looked really ill and Holly knew she needed medical attention – and fast. "Now, I'm going to turn my back to you and I want you to put your arms around my neck and hang on tightly. Like a piggyback. Can you do that?"

The girl nodded weakly. "I'll try."

"Okay." Holly was surprised at how heavy the girl was but she gritted her teeth and, very carefully and slowly, made her way back down from the ledge. It was hard work and she was terrified that she would miss her footing and fall, or that Sarah wouldn't have enough strength to hold on. Mercifully, despite a few scary moments, Holly's feet were soon back on the floor of the cave. Just a few more steps now, and they would be safely outside. By the time they emerged into the sunlight, Holly was out of breath and struggling to support Sarah's weight, so she had to let her slide down into the sand.

"Sarah, are you still awake?" she asked anxiously, crouching over the fragile girl.

58

"Yes, just about," she replied. "But I feel so strange and sleepy."

"You have to stay awake, just a bit longer," said Holly, getting her breath back. They had to keep talking. "How did you end up here?"

"It's a little hazy," Sarah replied. "I fell off my horse and he ran away. I hit my head and felt dizzy when I woke up and it was all dark. I got lost. So I just kept walking and then it started to rain and I was wet and this mist came. I was really scared, but a funny bird with a red beak kept swooping over me and keeping me company until I found the cave, so I sheltered here." She stopped to draw breath. "I climbed up on the ledge but then my head was still so dizzy, I had to lie down. Then when I tried to get up, I just couldn't move."

"Do you think you can stand up?"

"I'm not sure. I need my medication."

"I know."

The girl looked white and frail and Holly was really worried. They needed help. She reached into her pocket for her cell phone but it wasn't there. Had she dropped it somehow? Then the sickening realization hit her – she had left it in her bedroom to recharge the night before and forgotten to pick it up. She was on her own now.

"Okay, Sarah," she said calmly. "I need to get you up on my horse's back. I don't think I'm strong enough to lift you, but if you can stand on this rock, just for a second or two, I can push you into the saddle. Can you do that for me?"

Holly tried to support Sarah's weight while positioning the ever-patient Pumpkin close by. After some shoving and pushing, Sarah was finally sitting in the saddle and Holly climbed up behind her, arms around her waist to keep her from toppling forward.

The mist had completely cleared now and Holly hoped that she and Pumpkin would be able to find their way back. She was aware that the tern was circling above for the first part of the journey, which she took at a steady canter, but as soon as she recognized familiar territory the bird disappeared.

The household was just starting to stir when Holly clattered into the yard, shouting out for help. Suddenly her aunt and her cousins appeared, and Sarah was lifted gently from the saddle and laid on the sofa while Sam phoned for an ambulance.

"The heroine of the day – again," teased Anna, who stood beside her when, later, they watched the ambulance drive away. "We'll soon be dazzled by the light shining from your halo."

"Very funny," retorted Holly. Why did Anna always have to be so sarcastic?

But she didn't have any energy left to worry about Anna. All of a sudden she felt totally, completely exhausted.

Aunt Helena noticed that she could hardly stand on her feet and sent her to bed for a rest. She fell asleep almost before her head hit the pillow and didn't wake until late afternoon.

"Feeling better?" asked Aunt Helena when she wandered into the kitchen in search of fruit juice.

"Yes, thanks, though not very energetic."

"I'm not surprised. By the way, the police called and Sarah's parents want to thank you. You found her in the nick of time. Luckily, there's no serious damage done and she's making a good recovery."

"That's good news," said Holly, relieved.

Now that Sarah was safe, surely it would make a difference to Trojan's fate?

Chapter 7

"I'm going for a ride," Holly announced to Aunt Helena after breakfast the next day. "I need to see how Trojan is doing."

"No more adventures, though," said her aunt. "I'm very proud of you and so is your Dad, but I don't think we could cope with much more excitement."

Pumpkin seemed pleased to be out on the springy grass, taking bouncy strides as she trotted along the edge of the cliff. Sparrows chattered in the hedgerows and blue butterflies danced over the abundant sea-pinks that flowered along the cliff slopes. Holly was so preoccupied, however, that she hardly noticed.

Jordan heard the hoof beats as she rode up the path to Sedgewick and opened the big iron gates as she approached.

"Hey, Holly, I was going to call you." He sounded serious. "Bretton Riding Center called. They're in big trouble because of that girl."

"But she's been found and she's going to be okay – that's what I came to tell you."

"I know. I heard the news. You're a hero."

"It takes one to know one," she grinned. "So Trojan should get a reprieve, right?"

Jordan looked doubtful. "It's still bad publicity for the riding center. Even though, according to what they told Dad, she lied about her riding experience, gave them the impression she was a far better rider than she was, and went off on her own without telling anyone."

"So she's more to blame then they are," said Holly. "Surely that puts Trojan even more in the clear?"

"I can't see her admitting that, can you? Especially since it turns out her dad is a lawyer! Everyone will try to cover their tracks now. The riding center won't be able to sell Trojan now, so they don't want him back."

"You're kidding!" Holly looked puzzled. "You mean they're giving him to you?"

"No. They're not giving him to me. They're going to arrange for the vet to come over and put him to sleep."

"What?" Holly was aghast. "But they can't do that!"

"Yes, they can. Trojan is still their horse. They have to be seen as acting responsibly."

"But that's not being responsible – that's murder! Can't you buy Trojan off them?" asked Holly desperately.

Jordan shook his head and Holly noticed there was a sprig of straw sticking out of his jet-black hair. "We can't afford it. Besides, what if the girl's family found out the riding center had actually made money from this situation by selling the horse?"

Holly frowned. Reluctantly, she could see his point. "But there must be something we can do."

"Right now, the best we can hope for is to make Trojan's last few days good ones," Jordan replied. Holly swallowed hard. That sounded so final. It was horrible.

"The vet hates putting down a healthy animal, and he's told them the earliest he can do it is the end of the week, so we have three days left."

Three days to come up with a solution, decided Holly. There was no way, especially after risking her own life to save Trojan from the marsh, that she was going to let him die. No way.

"I can see you're upset," said Jordan gently, fixing her with his deep blue eyes. "How about we go out for a trail ride together, make the most of the rest of the day? You can leave Pumpkin here, give her a rest and ride Mercury."

In different circumstances, Holly would have jumped at the chance to ride out with Jordan, but right now she wasn't really in the mood. Even so, she found it hard to resist those haunting blue eyes so she shrugged and said, "Okay."

Mercury was sweet, with a broad back and comfortable, easy stride. Jordan rode beside her, chatting, and Holly tried to push Trojan out of her mind and enjoy the weather and company, but she didn't succeed.

"Sorry, Jordan, I just can't stop thinking about poor Trojan. It's so unfair."

"Me, too," said Jordan, pain evident in his voice. "Life can be so cruel sometimes." He sounded as if he was speaking from experience. They turned back to the house in silence.

As she rode away from Sedgewick later on, Holly felt desolate. Pumpkin, sensing her mood, plodded slowly and calmly, and by the time they got back tears were pricking at the corners of Holly's eyes as she untacked. She hoped her cousins were out riding because she hated the thought of their seeing her like this, but she was out of luck.

"Hi, Holl. Nice ride?" asked Sam, striding by

purposefully, her arms loaded with grooming tools, while Anna dangled a bridle from her shoulder.

Holly nodded, afraid to speak, hoping that Sam wouldn't notice. But Sam spotted her red eyes straight away. "Hey, what's wrong?"

Unable to prevent her voice from breaking, Holly blurted out, "They're going to destroy Trojan!"

Chapter 8

The twins were horrified when Holly explained what was going on.

"We have to do something," insisted Anna, her green eyes wide with anger.

"Like what?" replied Sam.

"Let's go to the hospital and get Sarah to admit it was her fault and that her bad riding made Trojan bolt."

"Anna, how exactly are you going to do that? Use your charm to persuade her?" said Sam sarcastically.

"If we make her realize that Trojan will die if she doesn't tell the truth…"

"Maybe it's worth a shot." Holly was glad to clutch at any straws to save Trojan.

"We have nothing to lose, and if she loves horses the way we do..." Anna sounded determined.

"What if she won't see us?" Sam was unconvinced.

"She'll have to see Holly, because she saved her life. So let's get over there."

"But the girl only just got admitted to the hospital. She probably won't be allowed visitors yet," Sam pointed out, fiddling with a strand of her short brown hair.

"I don't see why," said Anna doggedly.

"There's a tiny detail you may have forgotten, sis," said Sam. "Sarah has a heart condition. She's missed her medication, been trapped in a cave for two nights, suffering from exposure..."

"So we wait till this afternoon."

Sam groaned and made a face at her sister. "What do you think, Holly?"

"All I know is, we have to do something."

An hour later, Anna had phoned the local hospital and ascertained which floor Sarah was on and if she was allowed visitors.

"After 3p.m.. Family only."

"We're sunk," said Sam.

Anna smiled. "No, we tell them we're her sisters. And by the way, she's feeling much better."

Despite Sam's reservations, they caught the bus into town and set off together for the hospital.

"Third floor," said Holly, leading them into the elevator.

Sarah was sitting up in bed, in a small room in which she was currently the sole occupant, clearly surprised to see them. The color was back in her cheeks and she sounded cheerful.

"Holly, my rescuer," she smiled. "Thank you again."

"No problem," said Holly. "You remember my cousins, Anna and Sam?"

Sarah grinned. "How nice of you to visit me."

"We need to talk to you about what happened," said Anna, ignoring Sam's warning stare and diving in.

Sarah was taken aback. "There's nothing to tell. I went trail riding, the horse bolted, and I fell off. I don't remember much; it's kind of a blur. I kept passing out. Until Holly found me."

"Why did Trojan bolt? Did something scare him?" Anna persisted. "A car, or a plane or –"

"He just took off for no reason," Sarah insisted. "As I told my parents, he just went crazy."

Holly looked shocked. "You told your parents that?"

"Of course. Daddy is going to sue Bretton Riding

69

Center and probably put them out of business for good," she said with relish.

Sam groaned. "That will make things worse for Trojan."

Sarah looked puzzled. "I don't understand."

"You idiot, because of you an innocent horse is going to be destroyed." Anna sounded furious.

"Hey, that's not my fault."

"Why don't you just admit you fell off because of your bad riding?"

Sarah's mouth dropped open indignantly before her lip began to tremble. "That was a horrible thing to say. I've got a heart condition, you know." She reached her fingers toward her emergency buzzer. "I'm calling the nurse."

Sam said hastily, "We're so sorry to have upset you."

"Come on, time to go," said Holly, and she and Sam grabbed Anna's arm and pulled her away.

"But we haven't finished here," protested Anna.

"We're leaving now – before we get into more trouble."

They managed to get outside before the nurse appeared, but Anna was still seething.

"Well, that went well," said Sam sarcastically. "Well done, sis."

"I wanted to shake her," said Anna.

"Thank goodness you didn't." Holly sighed. "I think we just made things a whole lot worse for Trojan."

Chapter 9

They all caught the next bus back into town but Holly decided she wasn't going straight back to the B&B with her cousins. "I need time to think," she told them. "I'll be back later."

She sat on the wall by the harbor and took a few deep breaths as gulls soared and screeched overhead. What a fiasco. Holly was wondering what to do next when she noticed Jordan coming out of the grocery store across the road.

"Hi," she called out, waving to him.

He waved back and wandered over. "Can I join you?" he said. "You look annoyed. Bad day?"

"Awful," Holly replied and she told him about the disastrous visit to the hospital.

"That's a pain," he said. "Anna can be so hot tempered."

She was surprised at this remark. How well did he know Anna? She hadn't thought they were friends. But maybe they had more of a history than she had realized. An awkward silence followed before Jordan said, "Want some ice cream?"

They walked along the sea wall together, licking their cones and ducking the swooping gulls.

"So, how are you liking your summer vacation in Seashell Bay so far?" joked Jordan. "Or is that a silly question?"

"I like my aunt and the B&B. I love the bay. Pumpkin is sweet."

"What about the terrible twins?"

Holly smiled. "We didn't get off to a great start."

"Have you been homesick?"

"A little. I miss my dad and my sister, Claire. And my best friend, Jenni."

"What about your mom?"

"I don't have any contact with her. She left when I was little – after my sister's accident."

"I'm sorry. Do you want to talk about it?"

Suddenly Holly found herself confiding in him, as she explained about Claire's accident. "She got scalded when she pulled a kettle of boiling water over her face and arm. She was only six years old. It was my fault."

"Why do you say that?" Jordan asked softly.

"Because I was supposed to be keeping an eye on her but I didn't. I was watching my favorite TV show. My mom never forgave me, and I'm not sure if my dad has, either. But I'll never forgive myself."

"That sounds harsh."

"The irony is that Claire has always been okay about it. She never mentions the accident and we're devoted to each other. She's had skin grafts and stuff, and copes better now. Getting her horse, Samurai, helped her massively. Here's a picture of him," she said, pulling out her cell phone.

"He looks fabulous," said Jordan.

"He is," replied Holly. "Our golden horse."

"I think I told you Dynamite used to belong to my mother," said Jordan. "He's such a precious link to her."

"What happened to your mom?" asked Holly. She had opened up to him, so would he be able to do the same with her?

"I don't like to talk about it. I try to block it out." He hesitated, clearly uncomfortable. "But her death changed me. Partly guilt-driven, I suppose." His eyes were dark and haunted.

Holly sensed they had common ground, and for a moment, Jordan had seemed uncharacteristically vulnerable. He noticed the way she looked at him and seemed embarrassed. "Sorry to dump on you like that."

"It's okay to confide in someone," she replied.

"Not for me. Anyway, I need to get back, Dad will be home." He got up to leave and Holly wondered if she had somehow blown it again. But before he left he said, "Do you want to join me for a ride on the beach later?"

She smiled. "I thought you'd never ask."

That evening, as Holly rode Pumpkin to meet Jordan at the crossroads as arranged, she was still wrestling with the problem of Trojan's future, and determined that there must be a positive solution. She just hadn't figured it out yet, but she would, somehow.

Dynamite and Jordan looked impressive as they galloped up over the hill to meet her. Jordan smiled when he saw Holly, and they rode along the cliff path together, chatting like old friends. Although Holly still had lots of questions, she decided to save them for another occasion. Maybe she would try to pump her cousins for more information about Jordan when she got back.

They cantered down the winding path to the beach and let the horses cool their legs in the seawater. Later, just as the sun started to fade, they sat together side by side on the silvery sand, gazing out across the water in comfortable silence, while Dynamite and Pumpkin nuzzled each other nearby.

"I was wondering something," said Jordan, breaking the stillness.

"What is it?" Holly murmured dreamily, enjoying the closeness they were sharing.

"That girl, Sarah Parker. How did you find her? How did you know where to look?"

"I didn't. It was a complete fluke," she replied.

"Really? Sure it wasn't an instinct or sixth sense?"

Holly shook her head. "Nope. I did have some unexpected help, though."

Jordan was curious. "What do you mean?"

"I know it sounds crazy, but a funny-looking bird attracted my attention and led me along the beach to a bay that I might not have found otherwise."

Strangely, he didn't look surprised but just frowned. "Like the tern that hangs around Dynamite's stable?" He picked up a pebble and tossed it into the sea, watching it bounce across the water.

"Just like that bird. I thought it might even be the same one, though that would be stretching coincidence, wouldn't it?"

Jordan was silent and Holly noticed all the color had

drained from his face. "Are you okay?" she asked. "Did I say something to upset you?"

He stared at her, his eyes sad. Then he said darkly, "Why are you here?"

"What do you mean?" Holly replied, taken aback. He had a weird expression on his face and the tone of his voice made her uneasy.

"You know your cousins hate me, don't you? I bet they'd be furious if they knew where you were right now." He stood up and roughly grabbed Dynamite's reins.

"Hey, Jordan –"

"I can't talk about this. Your cousins are right, I'm trouble." He dug his foot into the stirrup and swung onto the black stallion's back. "Everything they say is true."

And before she could stop him, he rode away, leaving her alone and shivering on the empty cliff path.

Chapter 10

At supper that evening, Holly was still reeling from
Jordan's odd behavior. His tone had changed so abruptly,
it rattled her. What could she have said that upset him so
much? Maybe she didn't know him as well as she thought.

"What's up, Holly? You seem preoccupied," said Aunt
Helena, topping up the jug of orange juice.

"It's nothing. I'll be fine," Holly replied.

Anna peered up from her tuna salad. "Does it have to
do with Jordan, by any chance?" she asked smugly.

"It's none of your business," snapped Holly.

"It's just that we saw you out riding with him earlier."

Holly glared. "Were you spying on me?"

"Don't be an idiot. But we warned you that Jordan is bad news –"

"Why don't you zip it," muttered Holly, trying hard not to toss a bread roll at her annoying cousin.

"Now, girls, no arguing at the table please," said Aunt Helena. "I thought you were all getting along better now."

"We are, Mom," said Sam, smiling sweetly. "Honestly."

"Good," said Aunt Helena swiftly. "Now that we've finished eating you can help me wash dishes."

Afterwards, Holly wasn't in the mood to watch TV with the others so she went up to her room and lay back on her bed, gazing up through the skylight at the first glimmering stars. It certainly hadn't been a boring vacation in Seashell Bay so far, she had to admit. But she felt confused and disturbed about Jordan. What had made him change like that? What was going on?

There was a faint knock on the door.

"Only me," said Sam in a low voice. "Can I come in?"

Holly grunted but Sam pushed open the door and sat on the edge of the bed.

"You really like Jordan, don't you?" she said. "Has he upset you?"

"No," snapped Holly, determined not to discuss it with anyone, least of all her nosy cousins.

"He's not worth bothering about, believe me. Anyway, you must be really worried about Trojan."

Holly nodded. Sam was right. Her priority now was to save Trojan. "He only has two days left before… well, you know. I just feel so helpless."

"Anna and I have racked our brains, and short of spiriting him away, we're out of ideas."

Holly sighed. Why was life so full of problems? She felt tired. Several yawns later Sam said, "Okay, I take the hint. You want to sleep. Things will seem better in the morning. That's what Mom always says."

When Sam had gone, Holly decided to call her friend Jenni for some advice, but before she got the chance, her cell phone started to ring. To her surprise, it was Jordan. He sounded cool and distant, his tone matter-of-fact.

"I had a call from the riding center. Seems your visit to the hospital sparked a call from Sarah's lawyer Dad. So they're getting another vet in to do the deed tomorrow, first thing." He paused, waiting for her reaction. Holly was silent, too shocked to speak. "I know how much you care about Trojan so I just thought you ought to know, that's all. Night."

Holly lay the phone on the bed, stunned. This couldn't be happening. Despite her concern over Jordan, all she

79

could think about now was the lovely bay horse, safe and secure in his stable at Sedgewick, unaware that tonight would be his last. Tears filled her eyes and Holly knew what had to be done.

She waited until long after midnight, until the B&B was completely silent before she made her move. She wouldn't risk waking anyone by going down the stairs. Instead, dressed in black jeans and a sweatshirt, she climbed through her window and down the fire escape to the garden, thanking her lucky stars that Aunt Helena didn't keep a dog. She tiptoed across the lawn, constantly looking back over her shoulder to see if she was being followed or watched. At one point, she wondered if she saw a face at her cousins' bedroom window, but when she stared upwards, all she could see was a closed curtain. There was a full moon, which she thought was a double-edged sword. On the one hand, it lit her path up the cliff path toward Sedgewick. On the other hand, the bright silver light made her feel vulnerable and exposed to discovery.

She knew that there was a gap in the hedge that bordered the sides of the sprawling garden at Sedgewick and she managed to squeeze through it. She wasn't going to risk climbing the big iron gates. The stable block was a short walk now. Holly hardly dared breathe as each step took her closer, all the while expecting a security floodlight to home in on her and for loud alarm bells to wake everyone within a three-mile radius. She was nearly there now. She wanted the middle stable.

Carefully sliding back the bolts, Holly suddenly had a fear that the vet may have already been, that Jordan had got it wrong. What if she was too late? The second bolt clanged stiffly and she could hear Dynamite pacing in the stable next door, aware of the intruder.

"Easy boy, it's only me," she whispered reassuringly, dreading what would happen if he started to kick and make a fuss. He seemed to settle down and she opened the door to find Trojan standing in the far corner, resting a hind leg as he nibbled his hay net.

"We're going for a little stroll," she told him quietly, reaching calmly for his head collar, even though her heart was beating like a hammer inside her chest. He gave her a curious look, but allowed her to lead him outside into the damp night air, which he sniffed with interest.

Now for the difficult part. She couldn't get him through the gap in the hedge that she had squeezed through, and the iron gates were locked and over ten feet high. So how to get Trojan out? She had a plan, a simple one, but for Holly, it was the scariest part of her rescue mission.

"Okay, Trojan," she said, trying to sound confident and self-assured. "I'm breaking you out of prison, but you have to help me. I'm not a fearless rider like Jordan or my cousins. In fact, I'm a bit of a wimp and frankly would rather not gallop, let alone jump."

Her stomach lurched at the sound of the word but she continued. "Now, I'm going to get on your back, somehow, and I'm hoping you will be okay about that. You may have thrown Sarah, but let's face it, I did save your life and I'm doing it again, so you owe me now. Big time." Trojan lowered his head and gave her shoulder a friendly nudge. "Glad we got that sorted out," she said, grabbing a handful of mane and standing on a straw bale in the yard.

He stood calmly while she adjusted her position, gritting her teeth as she geared herself up for what she had to do. "See that hedge over there? The one I squeezed through? Well, Trojan, you're too big to do that so we're going to have to jump it. I know you can do it. I saw you tackle the railway crossing combination – remember? And it's not as high and there's no train hurtling toward us, so you should find it super easy." She squeezed her legs against his sides and, using the lead rope attached to his head collar, steered him toward the obstacle. He broke into a trot, and then a canter. For a moment, fear overtook Holly. This was not like the time she had galloped on Samurai, when she was racing to rescue her sister and best friend from danger, when she had been just as terrified but knew, deep down, that she was safe because Samurai was a special, amazing horse. Trojan, however, was not Samurai. He was stronger, and she had never even ridden him before. She could easily end up with a broken neck. Holly knew she had to control her fear, because as soon as Trojan knew how she felt, there would be no chance of controlling him. Focus, Holly, she told herself sternly. No time to be scared.

Trojan soon realized what she wanted him to do, and now they were only four strides away, then three, then two. Holly took a deep breath and gripped his black mane for dear life. "Here goes," she muttered, feeling the immense power of his hindquarters as he launched into the air, his forelegs reaching for the sky. Then they landed on the other side and she was still in one piece. Barely.

"Whoa, there, easy boy," she said firmly. If she didn't get him back in check, this was the time he would be most likely to bolt, when the adrenalin of the jump was pumping through his veins. But he came back to her willingly and to her relief slowed back into a steady trot, then walk. As soon as they were well clear of Sedgewick, she slid from his back and walked beside him. She knew exactly where to take him, somewhere he would be safe and no one would think of looking. Now all she had to do was find it again…

Chapter 11

Only four hours later, after all the other guests had gone out for the day, Holly was sitting alone in the dining room at the B&B, finishing her late breakfast, when Aunt Helena said, "Holly, hon, you've got a visitor."

Holly had half expected it but acted surprised when Anna added mischievously, "It's your boyfriend. So if I were you, I'd do something about the awful bags under your eyes because it looks like you didn't get any sleep at all last night." Her tone was uncomfortably knowing, which made Holly feel uneasy, but before she could pursue it, Jordan stormed in. "What did you do with him, Holly?"

" I don't know what you're talking about," Holly replied casually, sipping her tea, which seemed to infuriate Jordan further.

"Don't try and pretend. When the vet arrived this morning I had to tell him that the runaway horse ran away again."

"Really." Holly was determined to stay calm, even though she was aware of Anna hovering in the kitchen doorway nearby, eavesdropping.

"Where's Trojan?" Jordan's voice was raised and impatient. "If you don't tell me, it will only lead to more trouble – for all of us."

"I don't know what you're ranting about. I thought you were taking care of Trojan."

"I was." He glared angrily. "For heaven's sake, Holly." Then his tone softened. "I thought we were friends."

"So did I, until you went all weird on me."

"This is ridiculous. Holly, you are so going to regret this."

Suddenly Anna stepped in. "Don't you dare threaten my cousin. You're not welcome here, ever, so get out. Now."

Jordan opened his mouth, about to protest, but seeing that he was outnumbered he reluctantly turned and strode away.

"Thanks, Anna, but I can take care of myself," said Holly, a little annoyed at her cousin's behavior.

"I doubt that, since you still like him," replied Anna. "Besides, I meant what I said about him not being welcome here." She hesitated. "So, is he telling the truth? Did you take Trojan?"

"Of course not," replied Holly, aware that her face was reddening. It was clear that Anna suspected her and, knowing Anna, she wasn't about to give up until she found out exactly what was going on.

"Hmmm, well if I were you, I wouldn't want to be on the wrong side of Jordan." And with that, she walked away.

Holly knew she had to be extra careful now. She waited until her cousins went off for their customary morning ride before sneaking supplies from the kitchen and setting off to check on Trojan.

The beach was starting to fill up with vacationers, replacing the dog walkers and joggers that had used it several hours earlier. As she walked barefoot through the soft white-gold sand, her sandals slung over her shoulder, Holly breathed in the salt air and the smell of seaweed. She saw two of the local gray seals basking on a huge rock and another surfacing from the water at intervals between bouts of fishing. The bay was a truly lovely place to be. She passed by sea caves and arches as she put a distance between herself and the main beach until she reached a secluded bay – and the abandoned caves. Peering behind to check that she wasn't being followed, Holly stepped inside and scanned the huge cave for Trojan. Her heart missed a beat when she didn't see him at first. Then she heard a low nicker, and he turned as if to say, "Where's my breakfast?"

"Hey, Trojan. Sorry I'm a little late, but I have carrots and apples."

He gave a little snort and crunched noisily at her peace offerings. She started to relax, until she heard a familiar voice behind her. "You are such a bad liar, Holly."

"Anna! What are you doing here?"

"I could ask you the same question, little Miss Innocent. Wow, you were so easy to follow. But then I'm probably that much sneakier than you."

"Are you going to tell on me?" asked Holly, frustrated that she had been found out so soon.

Anna took a long hard stare at Trojan. "He is absolutely gorgeous, isn't he? You know, I keep replaying the way he jumped that railway barrier, just soared. He's destined for greater things than being a trail riding horse for stupid tourists."

"As long as no one finds him," replied Holly. "He's a fugitive now."

"Well, I won't tell. On one condition."

Holly sighed. "What's that?"

"As long as you agree that it's our secret."

Holly was surprised. "What about Sam?"

Anna said, "It's great being a twin. Most of the time. But people assume that you always want to do everything together and share everything. I am an individual, you know. And Sam would worry if she knew, and she'd find it really hard not to tell Mom, and then we'd be in trouble. So I'm not going to put her in that position. Deal?"

"I don't think I have a choice. Deal."

"Good. Now, as pretty as this cave is, I know a far better – and safer – place to hide a horse."

"Really?"

"Oh, yes. When Trojan has eaten his carrots, I'll take us there. Trust me."

Holly regarded her cousin with new eyes. Could she really trust Anna?

Chapter 12

Trojan crunched the rest of his breakfast noisily.

"So where is this new secret hiding place?" asked Holly.

"You'll see." Anna clearly enjoyed being mysterious and it seemed to Holly that she relished being part of an adventure.

"Shouldn't we wait until it's dark before moving him? What if someone sees us?"

"They won't," said Anna. "Not where we're going."

Holly wasn't sure whether to be anxious or relieved. Her anxiety was winning right now, but Anna was positively bubbling with excitement. "We can be there in twenty minutes."

With one girl each side of the horse, Anna took charge, grasping Trojan's head collar. "This way."

They set off toward the end of the bay, where the beach gradually ended, replaced by jagged rocks and boulders. When it seemed completely impassable, Anna stopped and headed for the chalk-faced foot of the towering cliffs.

"Where now?" said Holly. "This is a dead end."

"Not quite." Anna smiled. Behind a huge boulder, Holly saw a gap cut into the base of the cliffs. "We go through here."

"Through the cliffs?" Holly looked confused.

But Anna strode confidently forwards, with Trojan following meekly. Holly hurried after her and to her amazement she saw that a huge tunnel had been cut into the side of the cliff face.

"Wow!"

"Awesome, isn't it," grinned Anna. "I discovered it last summer, though it's been here forever. I bet it was used in the past by smugglers. We'll have to duck here and there, because the roof is low in spots. Try not to bang your head."

The tunnel twisted and turned and wound its way through the chalk, and Holly hoped that Anna knew where she was going. It was dark but Anna had brought a flashlight, clearly well prepared. Holly realized that Anna had planned to do this as soon as she suspected that Holly was hiding Trojan.

"Anna, are we nearly there? I'm getting a little claustrophobic," said Holly, the damp smell making her want to sneeze.

"Don't worry. Not much further."

"Where does it come out?" asked Holly.

"That's the best part," replied Anna, as the tunnel widened out and fingers of daylight began to filter through.

Holly was astonished when they surfaced to see that they were in the middle of the woods.

"Told you," exclaimed Anna triumphantly. "This will be Trojan's new home," and she pointed ahead, where a derelict old rental cabin nestled in the undergrowth, flanked by a freshwater stream. Holly blinked as her eyes readjusted to the bright sunlight, which felt dazzling after the darkness of the tunnel.

"No one will ever think to look here, so he'll be safe," said Anna confidently.

Holly patted the bay horse's silky black mane. "I hope so," she breathed. The girls tethered Trojan to an overhanging branch before clearing out the cabin.

"I come here now and then," explained Anna. "It's kind of a secret den. I haven't been for a while, and I don't think many people know where it is."

"Not even Sam?" wondered Holly.

"I haven't been here with Sam since last summer," replied Anna, checking the floor for anything sharp that might harm Trojan. When they were satisfied that it was hazard-free, Anna said, "We should probably get back now and return later with supplies."

"How are we going to sneak those out?" wondered Holly.

"We choose our moment carefully," replied Anna, and Holly wondered how much more of her cousin's cunning side would be revealed.

They went back through the tunnel and Anna explained that the hut could be accessed from the other side of the woods, but the dense undergrowth made it very difficult. She seemed reluctant to leave Trojan, but they both agreed to come back together after lunch.

Sam kept casting curious looks at Holly across the table while Aunt Helena chatted on about a new guest that was due to arrive shortly. Sam had been cleaning tack when they got back and had seemed surprised to see Holly and Anna arriving back at the B&B together. Holly was relieved that Sam didn't pursue it – for the time being. She hated lying, even if it was for a good reason, but the fewer people who knew about Trojan, the better.

Holly helped Aunt Helena clear up the dining room and lay it out for the evening meal while Anna and Sam offered to prepare the room for the new guest. Sam reappeared just before Holly had finished.

"All done, Mom, so I'm going to school Blackbird in the paddock for a while."

"Okay. Thanks for helping, girls," smiled Aunt Helena "Enjoy the rest of the day."

Holly followed Sam outside, expecting to find Anna in the stables with her sister, but there was no sign of her. Holly went back into the house to Anna's room, but it was empty.

Sam was practicing figure-eights at a neat collected canter when Holly got back outside.

"Have you seen Anna?" she asked.

"She's gone into town," replied Sam. "Said she had some shopping to do. A new pair of jeans or something. Left me to clean the bedrooms, the selfish thing." Her eyes were narrowed as she concentrated on her transitions, not wanting to be distracted by conversation.

Holly was puzzled. She and Anna had agreed to go back to see Trojan, so why had she gone off into town without saying anything? If she had gone into town, of course. Suddenly Holly felt annoyed. Knowing Anna, she had probably gone off to see Trojan on her own. It already felt like she was taking over. Seething, Holly set off briskly for the tunnel.

She managed to find it without any problems, but she didn't like walking through it alone. It was narrow and dark, and in her hurry and impatience, she had forgotten to bring a flashlight, which she very much regretted. Using the light from her cell phone, however, she finally made it to the other side.

"Anna," she yelled angrily, wanting to shake her cousin. But the hut door was wide open and when she peered inside, to her horror it was empty. Trojan was gone!

Holly began to panic. What if Trojan had been discovered? What if they had been unknowingly followed when they took him there that morning? She felt a flash of guilt. Maybe she had gotten Anna wrong after all. Maybe her cousin hadn't sneaked off to see Trojan by herself. Then Holly noticed the fresh hay net hanging up and the bucket of water. Holly frowned. So her gut had been right – Anna must have been here.

"Anna," she called again. "Where are you?"

She heard a faint but familiar voice in the distance, and she followed the stream into a sunlit clearing. Anna was already there with Trojan – and to Holly's annoyance, she was riding him. She wanted to storm

94

over and give her a good telling off for her selfish and thoughtless behavior, but she didn't want to spook Trojan, so she decided to wait until Anna was back on firm ground before saying what she thought. Anna, clearly oblivious and in a world of her own, was schooling the big bay horse, executing serpentines and circles at collected and extended trot and a perfectly balanced transition from walk to canter back to walk. Despite her frustration with her cousin, Holly had to admit that her cousin could ride. She couldn't help comparing Anna and Trojan to Sam and Blackbird, and it was plain that, as good a rider as Sam was, Anna had something special – especially with Trojan. Horse and rider seemed to have bonded. Holly felt a tinge of jealousy, but not for long. She was generous and mature enough to acknowledge that Anna and Trojan were far better matched than she was with the runaway horse, despite her affection for him.

Anna asked for halt and Trojan obliged obediently. Her face wreathed with smiles, Anna turned to Holly. "Isn't he just amazing?"

Holly nodded. "Yes, he is."

"He just needs a firm hand. I always said that Sarah girl couldn't have been riding him properly." She slid from the saddle and walked toward Holly. "I know I probably shouldn't have ridden him yet, but I just couldn't resist it. It's all I've been thinking about since we brought him here."

Holly tried to keep her face serious, still wanting her cousin to know she had been in the wrong, but it was hard when Anna was so full of enthusiasm, her green eyes alight.

"I haven't jumped him yet, although I'm dying to. It must feel great to jump on this horse."

Holly gave a mischievous smile. "It is."

Anna looked incredulous. "How would you know? Surely you haven't ridden him? Holly, have you really jumped Trojan?"

Holly nodded. "We jumped the hedge out of Sedgewick." She sounded casual but part of her felt good to have the edge on Anna for once.

"Oh, wow. Wow, Holly, I'm totally full of admiration. You are so full of surprises."

"I'm not the only one," said Holly pointedly.

Anna blushed. "Sorry."

"The question is, what are we going to do long term?" wondered Holly. "We can't hide Trojan forever."

"I know," agreed Anna. "But for the time being, until we think of something, let's just enjoy our time with him here. Please?"

Later that afternoon, when Holly was walking up the cliff path, alone, she felt glad that she had an ally in

Anna, who was clearly in love with Trojan. It felt odd keeping a secret from Sam, however, and she could see that would be difficult, if not impossible, to maintain. She had left Anna with Trojan, with Anna promising to return home soon so as not to arouse unnecessary suspicion. Deep down, Holly knew that this was very much a short-term solution. They would be discovered, sooner rather than later, she reflected, and Trojan needed to be in a real stable. She sighed. There had to be a resolution to this that would keep Trojan permanently safe, although she couldn't think of one yet. How hard would the authorities look for the horse? Would Sarah's dad just let the matter drop after time had elapsed, now that his daughter was recovering? Would the Bretton Riding Center be glad that the horse that seemed to have caused so much trouble was now off their hands, at least temporarily?

As she neared the top of the path, Holly hesitated. Her destination was in sight, but she was having second thoughts. She had decided earlier that she wanted to make her peace with Jordan. She couldn't leave things the way they were. They had to talk.

Sedgewick looked imposing, magnificent and mysterious, crowning the landscape, and Holly wondered why her cousins had said it was cursed. But it wasn't a place Holly would have wanted to live. There was a sadness, a coldness about it. She thought of the small house she shared with her father and Claire down a country road, how untidy it was, and noisy (when Claire was around) and warm and cozy. It was a home. Sedgewick was more like an ancient monument.

She decided not to announce her presence by ringing the bell at the big iron gates because if Jordan really didn't want to talk to her, he wouldn't let her in. Instead she went around the side and squeezed through the gap in the hedge. Dynamite was out in the paddock and Mercury was half-dozing over his stable door, so she knew Jordan hadn't gone out for a ride. Still, there were no familiar sounds of buckets clanking or yards being swept, and apart from the horses it was silent. This was going to be even harder now, she reflected. She would have to go up to the house. Taking a deep breath, she rang the booming doorbell. She waited for footsteps to echo down the hallway but there was no sound. She tried again. Nothing. There was no one home, it had been a wasted journey. With a heavy heart, Holly turned to go. Suddenly there was a scraping noise and the squeak of unoiled hinges and the heavy door swung open. Holly glanced back over her shoulder. Jordan was standing there, unsmiling, his blue eyes narrowed. His black thatch of hair seemed darker than ever.

"What do you want?" he demanded.

Holly swallowed. "Look, I hate feeling bad and I don't understand what I've done to upset you."

"You haven't done anything. Oh, apart from breaking into my stables and stealing Trojan," he said sarcastically.

Holly felt her face coloring. "Sorry. I meant the other day, when we were out riding together."

He stared back at her, but said nothing.

"Jordan, please talk to me. I thought we were friends. Oh, this is pointless, I don't know why I bothered even trying," she said impatiently, turning once to more to go.

"Wait," he called.

She stopped. "Yes?"

"I looked through the window and when I saw it was you, I wasn't going to open the door," he said.

"So why did you?"

He shrugged. "Maybe I wanted to explain something while I had still had the chance."

"I'm listening," she replied.

"Do you want to come in for a soda?"

They sat in the living room, Jordan on the sofa and Holly in the armchair, like the night he had rescued her. So much seemed to have happened since then.

"If you had met me a year ago you wouldn't have liked me at all," said Jordan.

"Why do you say that?"

"Because I wasn't a very nice person. I was always picking fights, I was a reckless rider, and I took stupid risks, just to get an adrenalin buzz. Dad and I were always arguing, and although Mom tried to keep the peace, I didn't show her a lot of respect either." He stared into his soda cup, as if embarrassed to look Holly in the eye. "The terrible twins didn't always hate me, you know. We were friends once. In fact, Anna liked my wild side."

He smiled ruefully. "We had a lot in common, then. But the crazier I got, the more worried Sam became, and it caused fights between them. It came to a head when I did something really stupid. We'd all gone out riding together, which we often did. I rode Mercury then, and he was already getting older and stiffer, and I got frustrated because I couldn't ride him the way I wanted to. Your cousins had set up a makeshift jumping course with logs and oil drums and they were both flying over on their ponies, Blackbird and Merlin. Anna had put some branches across these oil drums just before a big ditch to make a scary spread fence. Well, scary to Sam. Anna cleared it on Merlin, though, and she was looking pretty smug. Maybe it was that, or the fact that I knew Mercury couldn't do it. Sam just wimped out, got off Blackbird and said she wasn't going to overwork him and that we should call it a day; the ponies had worked hard enough. She was right, but I wanted to show off like Anna, and I knew Blackbird could clear it with a stronger rider, so I just snatched the reins from Sam, got on Blackbird and cantered him toward the jump. He wasn't ready, and I rushed it, and he ploughed through the branches and cut his legs really badly and landed in the ditch. There was blood everywhere and Sam was hysterical. Anna looked at me as if she hated me and I knew I'd gone too far. But I just made a stupid joke of it, tried to blame everyone but myself. Anna was screaming at me, and they somehow managed to get Blackbird home, but he was lame for weeks. It could have been far worse. After that, your cousins wouldn't have anything to do with me. Can't say I blame them, but at the time, I didn't want to take any responsibility for my actions."

He paused. "See, they were right about me."

"You're not like that now, though?" said Holly, reeling from what she had just heard. No wonder Sam and Anna held such a grudge. "So what changed you?"

"After that I just got angrier and more emotional, and one night I had a huge fight with Mom."

"What about?"

"Lots of things. Everything, really, I suppose. She was yelling at me about what had happened with Blackbird, because Anna had called her and told her and she got really upset. Mom was so gentle, wouldn't have hurt a fly, and the thought that her son could behave like that upset her. She said I was grounded. I just shouted back at her and stormed off. The weather was getting bad, heavy rain was forecast, and I knew she would be worried, so I stayed out really late, just to annoy her.

"By the time I got back, it was starting to get dark. Dad was waiting for me, furious, but Mom wasn't there. Despite the fact that she hadn't been feeling well, she'd taken Dynamite and gone out to look for me. She was worried. Dad tore into me, and we had another fight. I knew I had to apologize to her. I dreaded having to face Mom when she got back."

He paused. "But she didn't come back. So I never got the chance to tell her how sorry I was." His voice was quivering. "Dad and I were still shouting at each other when Dynamite returned – alone. We realized something bad must have happened to Mom. I'll never forget that moment. We went out to look for her. The alarm was raised, and the local community formed a search party, Anna and Sam included. Everyone loved my Mom. She was the kindest person ever."

"It must have been awful."

"Words can't describe it. It was the worst week of my life. When 24 hours had passed and the police hadn't found her, we kept telling ourselves it would be okay, that she'd turn up soon, as if nothing had happened. As the hours turned into days, the hope began to drain away. They

102

found Mom's body in the sea a week later. The police said she must have fallen off the cliff. The postmortem said she died instantly. Dad was inconsolable. He never accused me, but I knew he must have thought that if I hadn't argued with her that night, she would still be here now. I thought the guilt would tear me apart. That's when I resolved to change, to be a better person. Too late, of course. I don't deserve a second chance."

Holly was overwhelmed with sadness. She knew exactly how it felt to carry such a burden of guilt around. Jordan must be very lonely. She wished she could help him but in tragic circumstances like this, she knew there was nothing she could say.

"Dynamite is so important to me," continued Jordan. "He's the only link I still have to my mother. And he was the only witness to what happened that night, the only one who knows." He smiled ruefully. "Maybe the reason I go out riding at night is because I'm looking for answers, hoping that somehow it will get me closer to the truth."

Holly reached out and took his hand. "It's okay," she said, wanting to comfort him.

"No, it's not okay. It will never be okay again." But he let his hand rest in hers and they sat in silence for a while, listening to the ticking of the clock.

"You should go home before it gets any later," he said.

"There's a storm forecast and they say it will be a bad one. There will be mist on the cliff path soon."

Holly stood up, unwilling to leave him alone like this. As if reading her mind he said, "I'll be fine. Dad's due home any minute. Don't worry. I'm glad we talked."

"Me too."

"Be careful on the path," he said, opening the door. "By the way, no point in me asking about Trojan, I suppose?"

She hesitated. He had confided in her in a way she hadn't expected and part of her wanted to share the secret. But for now, she had to keep it to herself.

"He's safe," she replied.

"For now. Night, Holly."

It had been another eventful day, Holly reflected, as she hurried back to the B&B. The mist had already begun to descend when she arrived back and there was a chill in the air and an uncomfortable dampness.

"Oh, Holly, I've been waiting for you to get back," said Sam, rushing out to meet her. She looked frantic with worry. "Something terrible has happened!"

Chapter 13

Sam grabbed Holly's arm and hurried her out to the stables so they could talk in private. Holly was immediately alarmed. She had never seen her cousin like this before.

"Sam, what's wrong?" she asked, trying to keep her voice calm.

"It's Anna. I think she's run away."

Holly was taken aback. When she had left the woods earlier with Trojan, Anna had promised to come back home. Had she gone on the run with Trojan? "When did you last see her?" she asked, panicking.

"About an hour ago."

"An hour?" So Anna must have been back since Holly left her.

Sam nodded. "We had a huge fight."

"What about?"

"Trojan."

Holly's heart sank again. Was it time to confess or did Sam already know?

"I found Anna's diary," explained Sam. "Well, not exactly found, I mean, I know where she hides it. And I know I shouldn't have looked, but she has been acting so strangely recently. She walked in on me while I was reading it and went crazy. I hadn't seen much, just the last entry, about riding Trojan, so I guessed she must have taken him and hidden him somewhere. I told her she had to give him back or she'd be in big trouble."

Holly was shocked. She wondered what else Anna had written in the diary – and how much more Sam knew.

"She said she wasn't going to give him back – ever. Then she snatched the diary back and just stormed out."

"Does Aunt Helena know about this?" asked Holly uneasily.

"Not yet. But I'll have to tell her now, won't I?"

Holly's mind raced. Once her aunt knew what was

going on, it would definitely be the end for Trojan, so they had to find Anna before it all got out of hand.

"I think I know where Anna might be," said Holly.

"Let's go, then." Sam grabbed a flashlight and the two girls set off for the beach.

"So where are we going and why do you think you know where to find my sister?" asked Sam curiously. Holly realized that Sam had really not had the chance to read much of Anna's diary.

"To the old rental cabin," replied Holly, waiting for the reaction.

Sam was stunned. "How do you know about that? It was our secret place. Well, it was supposed to be, although we haven't been there for ages now."

"Anna took me," replied Holly. "It's where she suggested we hide Trojan."

"We?" The hurt in her tone was evident.

"Look, Sam, I'm sorry. This is really awkward. I horse-napped Trojan to save him from being put down and hid him in a cave. Anna followed me there and persuaded me to move him to the place she thought would be safer. I had to go along with it. Trojan's welfare was my priority."

"I understand that," replied Sam. "I just would have expected –"

"Anna would have told you. I know. Me too."

They walked on in silence for a while, a white mist descending over the choppy sea. Holly wasn't looking forward to being in the tunnel, but when they got there, Sam took the lead with her heavy-duty flashlight to light their way. By the time they emerged at the other end, it was no longer golden sunlight that greeted them, but a blanket of gray as the sky darkened rapidly.

"Anna, where are you?" called Sam, her voice a mixture of anger and fear.

There was no reply. The hut was empty. Holly started to call too, and they ventured from the woods into the clearing, but an eerie silence engulfed them.

"I don't think she's here," said Holly.

"So where is she?" Sam was getting worried and Holly wondered if Anna really had run away with Trojan. Thunder began to rumble in the dark clouds overhead and a flash of lightning suddenly forked across the sky. Then the rain started, softly at first, but quickly gathering pace until it was lashing down.

"We've got to find her," said Sam. "She can't have gone far. She didn't have much time on us."

Holly considered, then said, "If you were Anna and you wanted to take Trojan away, where would you go? Keeping in mind that you don't want to be seen."

Sam thought for a moment. "Through the woods, but not out on the side where it meets the road. There's a way out through a winding path, just past the clearing, that takes you back up to the cliff tops." She shuddered. "But in these conditions, the trail along the cliffs would be treacherous. If Trojan slipped and missed his footing…"

"Come on," Holly said decisively. "Let's find her."

By the time they had scrambled up the trail to the cliff top, both girls were soaked through and soon enveloped by the blanket of mist.

"There was one more thing I read in Anna's diary that really shocked me," said Sam suddenly.

"What's that?" asked Holly uneasily.

"She still cares for Jordan."

Holly felt as if she had been hit by a lightning bolt, but before she could pursue Sam's revelation, they heard a terrified whinny as another clap of thunder resounded over the bay.

"Look, over there." Holly followed Sam's pointing finger to see a horse standing by the edge of the cliff. It was Trojan. And he was riderless.

"Oh, no," whispered Holly. It was as if history were repeating itself, but this time it was Anna who had been thrown by Trojan and not Sarah Parker. This time her own cousin was missing.

"Anna!" screamed Sam, running toward the loose horse.

"Slow down, you'll freak him out," warned Holly,

catching Sam's arm. Sam stopped in her tracks and took a deep breath. Taking careful steps, both girls approached Trojan with caution, but he seemed glad to be reunited with human company especially Holly, who he nuzzled gratefully.

"Easy, boy," she soothed. "What have you done with your rider?"

"Anna," Sam kept calling, but no familiar voice echoed back at her. It was then that Holly noticed the dark shape lying on a ledge at least ten feet down from the cliff top, jutting out above the rocks and crashing waves below. She gestured to Sam, who shone her flashlight down at the ledge. The figure was lying awkwardly, one leg at a strange angle, but they both recognized Anna's patterned yellow tee shirt in the flashlight light. Sam switched the flashlight to its most powerful beam, shining it onto Anna's upturned face. There was blood across her forehead and her eyes were closed. The light flickered as Sam's hand shook with fear.

"Tell me she's alive, Holly," she murmured tearfully.

But Holly couldn't answer at first. "She must be unconscious," she said uncertainly.

"Anna, wake up!" shouted Sam desperately. But Anna didn't respond. "She looks badly hurt," said Sam. "We need help."

Holly tried her cell phone but they both knew there would be no signal where they were.

"We can't get her without help; she's too far down, and it's much too dangerous," said Holly. She glanced up across the skyline. The nearest house was Sedgewick.

"You'll have to ride for help," said Sam.

"Me?"

"Well, I'm not leaving my sister."

Holly hesitated. She looked at Trojan standing beside her, the rope from his head collar dangling. They didn't know how Anna had ended up falling over the cliff. What if Trojan had bolted with Anna and thrown her? Anna was a strong rider. If she couldn't control him what chance did Holly have?

Sam said desperately, "You have to get help, Holly. You must."

Holly knew she was right. There was no time to lose. She reached for the rope but Trojan immediately threw his head up, eyeing her suspiciously. Maybe he'd had enough for tonight? Or perhaps he sensed her anxiety?

"I can't," she said, panicking.

"You've got to. Please, Holly. I have to stay with Anna."

Holly understood perfectly. If it were Claire lying injured down there, she would feel exactly the same. Come on, she told herself, you rode him once before, you jumped him over the hedge. With a determined look, she approached Trojan again and although he still shied away, she took the rope firmly and mounted. She could feel him tense beneath her. Another flash of lighting made them both jump and he reared up. He was as scared as she was. When she realized that, Holly felt calmer. They had to work together. "Come on, boy," she said gently. But Trojan was still sidestepping and Sam gave her a nervous glance, clearly wondering if there would be more casualties that night.

"Don't worry, Sam, I'll get help," Holly reassured her. She squeezed the horse's sides and he shot forward straight into a canter, banging her face on his neck. Going too fast in this weather could be fatal, so Holly pulled hard, trying to get him back under control. Eventually he responded and she steered him toward the path that led to Sedgewick.

Once they were away from the cliff top, she squeezed harder and he increased his pace. For a moment, she felt okay, but then realized that Trojan was getting too fast for comfort for her. Holly clung on, trying at intervals to regain control, praying he didn't catch his foot in a rabbit hole and trip. He was galloping madly now and Sedgewick was in sight. She couldn't stop him so she had to try and steer instead. Trojan still kept up the crazy pace and then she remembered the gates that would be locked.

She wouldn't be able to stop him in time and they were far too high to jump.

Thinking fast, Holly changed course and veered him toward the hedge, which he'd jumped before. "You can do it," she muttered, to herself rather than Trojan. He didn't decrease his pace and was going much too fast. He rushed the jump, taking great chunks of the hedge with him and stumbling on landing. Holly went flying over his head, rolling herself into a ball to protect herself, tucking her head and hands in. This must be what it feels like to be a hedgehog, she thought when she eventually stopped rolling. When she peered up, Trojan was lying crumpled on the ground and her heart missed a beat.

"Trojan? No!" Had she killed him by making him jump?

Suddenly floodlights caught her in their glare and she heard voices and saw Jordan and his father running toward her. "Holly, are you okay?"

She nodded, gasping and pointing. "Trojan."

They stared, horrified, at the horse lying there, neck outstretched. Holly felt sick. Poor brave Trojan. She felt tears welling up. She had pushed him too hard. Then, without warning, they heard a low whicker and the horse shuddered as he clawed back to his feet and shook himself violently.

"Is he alright?" Holly was standing too, now, ignoring

the pain in her bruised arms as they both rushed over to the horse. Trojan lifted his head and snorted. Jordan slowly took the rope and tentatively walked the horse a few steps, convinced that he would be limping, but to their relief Trojan moved normally.

"This horse has nine lives," sighed Jordan.

"Thank goodness. But we have to help Anna."

Holly blurted out what had happened, the words tumbling out of her mouth like a waterfall. Jordan's dad took charge of Trojan while phoning the rescue services on his cell. Jordan quickly tacked up Dynamite and vaulted into the saddle. He reached out his hand to Holly. "Come on, you have to show me where Anna is." Her legs felt like jelly, but Holly grasped his wrist firmly and he whisked her up behind him on the saddle.

"Hold tight," he instructed. Wrapping her arms around Jordan's waist, Holly pressed her face against his back as they galloped up the cliff path.

Dynamite raced against the wind, and if wasn't for the fact that they were riding to save Anna, Holly would have enjoyed being so close to Jordan. For now, however, she had to concentrate, to remember the way back, and in this heavy mist, and under pressure, it wouldn't be easy.

"Turn left," she shouted, as the path ended, but to their mutual dismay, the path came to a dead end.

"Which way now?" asked Jordan.

Holly scanned the horizon, searching for a landmark, but it all looked so different now, swathed in thick mist.

"I don't know." The words were heavy with despair. This was no time to get lost. Then Holly glimpsed a big wraith-like bird outlined by a fuzzy silvery haze, hovering in the other direction.

"That way," she said, wondering if Jordan had seen what she had. She was fairly sure from his reaction that he hadn't noticed. Dynamite raced gamely onwards and they soon found their way back to Sam standing on the cliff top, utterly distraught.

"Hurry. Anna's lying right on the edge," cried Sam. "She woke briefly but she doesn't know where she is and she rolled over. I was sure she'd go over the ledge. I kept calling but she just closed her eyes again. What if the rescue service doesn't get here in time? If she falls, it's a hundred-foot drop!"

They all stared down onto the treacherous rocks below, the sea wild and menacing, the wind howling. Holly glanced across at Jordan, who must surely have been reminded at that moment of what happened to his mother. Suddenly he said firmly, "Don't worry, Sam, I'll make sure she doesn't fall."

And to their horror, before anyone could stop him, Jordan had disappeared over the edge and begun to climb down the craggy cliff face.

"You're crazy, Jordan, you'll be killed," shrieked Holly.

He kept going, and as they watched, petrified, he managed to get nearer and nearer to the ledge where Anna was trapped.

"He's almost there," breathed Sam, at which point Jordan missed his footing and nearly slipped. Holly's heart was in her mouth. This was like a bad dream.

Jordan recovered his foothold, and then he was crouching on the ledge, with barely enough room for both of them. Anna lay motionless and he cradled her head, telling her everything would be alright while the rain beat down on them. Mesmerized, Holly felt frozen by cold and fear.

When, at last, the rescue services helicopter arrived, she imagined that the loud clattering in the sky was simply more thunder. Her hands felt so numb she could no longer feel her fingers.

Sam traveled in the ambulance with Anna, who was still lying unconscious on the stretcher, her face ashen. Jordan insisted that the scratches on his hands and arms were superficial and was allowed to ride back on Dynamite. Holly rode behind him again. She wanted to stay with Jordan.

"You were amazing," she told him.

He shrugged. "Anyone would have done the same.

Besides, I'm an experienced rock climber so it wasn't the risk it seemed to be."

"It was so brave," she said, resting her head against his back as Dynamite trotted along the track to the B&B. Aunt Helena was getting in the car to drive to the hospital when they arrived and Holly promised to keep an eye on things until she got back.

"Sorry to ask a favor when you've had such an awful night," said her aunt. "But I trust you completely."

"Thanks."

"And Lena will help if there are any problems."

"Don't worry."

Holly waved her aunt away. "Will you come in, Jordan, at least for a while?" she asked.

He shook his head. "I should get back." Holly reached forward to give him a little kiss on the cheek. "Thank you," she said. He looked at her and for a moment, she wondered if he would return the kiss. Just then, there was a commotion from the B&B and she heard Mrs. Clayton and her son arguing loudly.

"Come back here, Ross," his mother shouted, but the boy pushed his way past Holly and outside into the yard. Holly was about to tell the boy off for his rudeness when Ross suddenly stopped in his tracks. He went as white as a sheet, taking a step back. He stared at Jordan. "It's him," he murmured, his voice shaking with fear. "He was there, that night."

Holly was puzzled and Mrs. Clayton looked equally confused.

"What do you mean?"

"The night the woman fell over the cliff. He was there. And I saw what happened."

Chapter 14

"I don't know what you mean," said Jordan. "What are you talking about?"

"It was a year ago, but I still recognize him," the boy persisted, walking forwards, pointing his finger.

Holly stared at Jordan in disbelief. What was Ross saying? Was it really true, that Jordan had caused his mother's death?

"But I wasn't there," protested Jordan.

"Not you," said the boy, reaching out to touch

Dynamite. "Him. The black horse with the funny shape on his face. Her horse."

Holly and Jordan exchanged surprised glances.

"What did you see, Ross?" his mother prompted gently. "You need to tell us."

"I'm scared," he replied anxiously.

"I always wondered if something happened when we were here last, because you've been so withdrawn since," said Mrs. Clayton. "But you refused to talk about it. We want to help, Ross."

Holly nodded encouragingly, although she was as mystified as Jordan.

Reassured, Ross continued, "It was getting dark and misty. I'd gone for a walk and got a bit lost. This lady rode past me, asked if I was okay. She was pretty. She smiled, although she looked upset. She said she was looking for her son."

Jordan went pale as he heard this.

"She rode beside me for a while and showed me the way back. Then she saw a bird and it was flapping and hurt. It was on the cliff ledge and its leg was caught in wire. She said she was going to rescue it. She got off her horse and I held him for her while she climbed down. I was worried that it looked dangerous but she got to the bird and she freed its leg. But as she turned she slipped. I shouted to warn her but it was too late. She fell." His voice was shaking. "I looked over the edge but I couldn't see her. It was too far. All I could see was the water and rocks. I was so scared."

There was total silence as the boy continued. "I held her horse after it happened, and I was crying. Then the bird flew off and made the horse jump so he ran away too."

"Ross, why didn't you say anything about this at the time?" asked his Mom.

"Because it was my fault. I should have saved her."

"You were a child. How could you have saved her? Oh, Ross."

"I'll never, ever forget that night," he sobbed. "I keep dreaming about it."

Jordan suddenly said calmly, "Ross, what kind of bird was it?"

The boy wiped his eyes. "A silver-gray bird, with a black mark on its head. Funny looking thing. With a bright red beak."

A week later, Holly was riding Pumpkin for the last time on her way to Sedgewick.

The sun was shining and it was hard to imagine that the cliff tops and beach, now drenched in sunlight, could ever be threatening and dangerous.

Anna was back from the hospital, nursing a broken leg and a concussion. She had fumed for a while because she wouldn't be able to ride for the rest of the summer, but Sam reminded her she was lucky to be alive, and she calmed down. Holly had wondered if the sisters would be able to repair the rift that had been created between them. Sam had clearly felt betrayed by Anna over the matter of keeping Trojan and the old rental cabin a secret. Now she felt sure that time would heal these wounds, since Sam had hardly left her sister's bedside for the first night at the hospital. There was still the problem of what to do with Trojan, although Aunt Helena had cleverly suggested they offer a donation to a charity of Sarah's choice in return for keeping him, and that offer had been positively received by Sarah's family. Maybe Anna would get to keep Trojan after all? Holly had to admit they made a good team, especially as it turned out Trojan hadn't bolted with Anna after all; he had just been spooked by the thunder and lightning.

As she neared Sedgewick, Holly's thoughts turned to Jordan, to the way he had looked at Anna when she had been carried out on the stretcher, and how he had risked his life for her. Deep down, she knew he still had a soft spot for Anna, although he was too stubborn to admit it. So he and Anna had a lot in common!

"Hey, Holly," he called, as he met her at the big iron gates on Dynamite. "It's the last day of your vacation, right? Better make the most of the sun."

They rode off side by side, the horses ambling quietly, and birds singing overhead. "Holly, can I ask you something?"

"Sure, go ahead."

"That bird, the one who keeps hanging around Dynamite and Sedgewick. Do you think it's the same one that my mother tried to save?"

Holly considered this. "I know it might sound a crazy, but I wouldn't be surprised."

"I kind of think that too," he replied. "Like it's trying to say thank you. There was something my mom said once, a long time ago. She told me that at the end of her life she hoped she could just fly away, free as a bird."

"Do you think that your mom's spirit lives in the bird she rescued?"

"I'd like to believe that," he replied, his tone bittersweet.

"Anna and Sam said that Sedgewick was cursed," Holly said suddenly. "Do you think so?"

"The place has certainly had its share of bad luck," agreed Jordan. "My ancestors were all victims of misfortune of one kind or another and there have been too many tragedies over the years."

"Maybe it's time to move on," Holly suggested.

"Dad was talking about selling, before Mom died. He's seen a cottage across the bay, which he says would be perfect. Not far from the B&B."

Or Anna, Holly smiled to herself.

"I'll miss you, Holly," he said. "You're a good friend."

"You too," she replied, knowing it could never be more than that. "My hero."

He laughed. "My heroine. I think we saved each other."

"Well, I'm glad you and my cousins have made your peace together," she said. "And I can go home knowing that Trojan will have a good home."

Home. The word made Holly feel warm inside. She couldn't wait to see Claire and Jenni and Samurai. She had missed them.

And the summer was only half over – there'd be plenty of time to read and relax. No jumping. No galloping. And definitely no more adventures.